THE RAZOR'S EDGE

K A R L   J I R G E N S

THE RAZOR'S EDGE

The Porcupine's Quill

Library and Archives Canada Cataloguing in Publication

Title: The razor's edge / Karl Jirgens.

Names: Jirgens, Karl, 1952– author.

Description: Short stories.

Identifiers: Canadiana (print) 20220173168 | Canadiana (ebook) 20220173176
    | ISBN 9780889844506 (softcover) | ISBN 9780889844513 (PDF)

Classification: LCC PS8569.I74 R39 2022 | DDC C813/.54—dc23

1   2   3   •   24   23   22

Published by The Porcupine's Quill, 68 Main Street, PO Box 160,
Erin, Ontario NOB 1TO. http://porcupinesquill.ca

Edited by Stephanie Small. Represented in Canada by Canadian Manda.
Trade orders are available from University of Toronto Press.

We acknowledge the support of the Ontario Arts Council and the
Canada Council for the Arts for our publishing program. The financial
support of the Government of Canada is also gratefully acknowledged.

This book is for you, because now's the time.
And this book is for those who have come and gone.
And this is for all the fools who ever were.
You are all loved more than this humble
and unprolific voice can say.

When will we learn the difference
between turning on people
and turning people on?

TABLE OF CONTENTS

I believe it was Franz Kafka who once said
that a book must be an axe
that breaks the frozen sea within us.

—KJ

PRELUDE:
CINDERELLA PECADILLA

Even years later, I remember the dream exactly. I was standing in front of my house on Rivercrest Road in Toronto. I haven't lived there for years. But that dream remains lucid. I was standing before my house, and for no particular reason, was looking south. My house is on the east side of the street, and Rivercrest Road follows a ridge adjacent to the Humber River. It was an ordinary day, mild, with sunshine breaking through the oaks. A light breeze caressed the treetops. It was a blue-sky day spackled with white clouds. I gazed down the street to see a sole figure moving towards me along the eastern sidewalk. I squinted but could only make out that the person had shoulder-length brown hair and wore a loose white gown. I gazed north and saw that I was otherwise alone. I turned south again. The figure was closer, except it seemed to be hovering rather than walking. It may simply have been the way the white robe stirred in the breeze. I looked more carefully. A wave of recognition swept over me. Soft, long brown hair, a flowing white robe and a red mark on the chest. At first, I thought he was injured. As he drew closer, I saw that the colour red arose from an open heart, glowing, aflame, encircled by thorns. I realized that it was Jesus approaching. I felt as though I was enveloped in a magnetic field of sorrowful waves and unconditional love, a sad joy. I was to have a reckoning. And then, the telephone rang.

It was Sarah, who calls me from time to time, to use me as a sounding board, and I'm always annoyed because she talks at length and I can't get a word in edgewise. I wanted to curse her for awakening me from my dream, but instead, I cursed the devil and the telephone company for the intrusion. Her greetings were always perfunctory. Her aim was to unload baggage, unburden herself. I contemplated the irony of a troubled Jewish woman calling me just as I was about to meet Jesus. I sensed that she was on edge, but I needed help, too. I thought about the heart encircled by thorns. I felt a contrite joy, a blessed shame. I was messed up, making foolish mistakes, influenced by the wrong kinds of people. Without pause, Sarah raged about her sad existence. I pretended to listen but remained unfocused. It occurred to me that Jesus was Jewish too. There had to be a reason for her phone call. I tuned in to her tirade but remained of two minds. I was furious that she had broken my dream but flattered that she had chosen me, trusted me. Over the past couple of years, she called sporadically, at unpredictable times of day or night. I'd listen, and threaten to use her words in a story, to which she'd reply, 'Go ahead! Use me in a story! I love it. I've got a strong Leo influence, and Leos love it when you talk about them.' She was telling me about her broken marriage, her crazy lovers, the comedian she'd been seeing off and on who wasn't very good at sex, but she wanted to keep seeing him anyway. 'He can't even get it up! I had to tie him up and blindfold him, and he kept touching *himself* instead of me.'

I wanted her to shut up but couldn't help listening. Her voice was self-mocking. Sad, but flippant. Proud but embarrassed. From past encounters, I knew that she was private, but revealed everything as a routine matter.

'And after two minutes, it was all over. Not like the man from the night before—he was really good, really knew how to do it, you know? But I got friction-burn from that guy, and it wasn't that pleasant anymore, but he was knowledgeable, knew what made you feel great, but after a while it was just exercise, and I'm not into any sexual Olympics, you know what I mean? In the morning I noticed that he was wearing a swastika ring, and this bothered me a lot, even if he was good looking and good in bed. He said he'd call me later, but he never did. Anyway, it was my way of dealing with the comedian. This way, he wouldn't get a strong emotional hold on me. I don't want to get trapped. I'm always of two minds on these things and I can't ever decide what's best. What bugs me is I've been trying to get my life organized lately, so I've been seeing this psychologist for about two weeks, and I let it drop about this guy with the swastika ring, and suddenly she gets hostile. She asks me what my goals are, so I tell her I want to turn out a book, not just a little chapbook, but a real book from a halfway respectable press, and I tell her I want to do a CD, not just another crummy EP from some fly by night company, but a decent label, you know? And she looks at me and says, "My aren't *we* ambitious?" Like I could never do it in a million years, see? I mean, she's my *psychologist*! I'm supposed to get *therapy* from her!'

So, I told Sarah that it was a good idea to try for a book or a CD, because it might generate that Cinderella moment she was looking for. And I told her I thought that she was a sucker in relationships. She'd be better off on her own, at least for a while. And, without telling her, I thought of the world of dreams, and how in a dream a million years can be a split second. Or, a minute can take a lifetime. And I wondered if I would ever have another dream with Jesus.

'And then my shrink says she doesn't think she can handle my case, because I'm too screwed up. She says that my problems began years ago, and it would take too long to straighten me out.

So, I asked her if she would say the same thing if I hadn't mentioned the guy from the night before, and she's suddenly quiet, and she looks like she hasn't had it in years, you know what I mean? Not that I'm especially promiscuous myself—I mean I haven't had a decent relationship for a year and a half, but I don't need that kind of negative reinforcement, especially from somebody who's supposed to be helping me, some *psychologist*. I'm neurotic enough already, and the comedian isn't helping any. He claims he loves me, but I know it's not true because all he wants is his idea of kinky sex. I mean, he doesn't even phone me unless he gets drunk and horny. I wanted him to call me just so I could yell at him and say, "Don't ever call me again!" And finally, he did call, and I said, "Who do you think I am, your *call* girl?" And he said, "No. You're my *no* call girl, because I know you don't want me to call you." What a twist O. He kind of reminds me of Matt, you know, the guitarist? He's always trying to pounce on me when I'm at his place, but he behaves when we're at my place, because he gets all weirded out and quiet, so I do all the talking because somebody's got to do the entertaining, and at least that way I'm not bored.'

So, I said, 'Are you telling me all of this because you're bored? Are you entertaining yourself? Why did you call me, anyway?' And she said, 'Listen, I don't know what to do or who to turn to. My shrink's a dead loss, and you're pretty level-headed, not like those other creeps. I was thinking maybe I could use you for a sounding board.' So, I told her it was okay, and she barged on.

'So, I tell him, "Matt, you know we can never fuck, not after the way things have gone in the past." So instead, he wanted a massage, so, I massaged his hands for a whole hour. He really liked that. His fingers always hurt from playing guitar. He has nice hands, but they're very feminine, I guess he keeps them in shape from his guitar playing. Anyway, they're too feminine for me. I wouldn't want them touching *my* naked body. But he liked it when I massaged his fingers. Then, he wanted a head massage, like, he wanted me to massage the bumps on his head, you know? So, I was a little weirded out, but I did it for a while, and he's got plenty of bumps too, and he started to say how good it felt, so I told him to forget about it, because that was all the head he was going to get from me. He's got sex on the brain. Like, three years ago, when I wouldn't go to bed with him, he asked me what I wanted, so I told him to go down on me while I was standing up. It was a *joke*, you know, but he did it anyway. And *now* he wants to go through the same old thing again, and I know he doesn't love me. All he wants is sex. He doesn't even care for me, but he's got the hots for me, I'm sure. I mean he's hard every time I'm near him. So anyway, I'm sitting around his place, and I get hungry. I'm getting more independent lately, you know? I'm starting to take care of myself, so I go to the store and buy some eggs, and I take them back, and Matt says, "You can't cook those here, get them out of here, I can't stand eggs." So, I said, "Look-it, I'm hungry and I'm not going to sit here and drink orange juice while I pass out." That whole week I felt like I had *anorexia nervosa* on account of the way things were going, so I made a kind of omelette thing, but I was nervous and put in too much oil. They could've turned out better, but they were okay, and while I'm sitting there eating, he goes, "Yech, I hate eggs, make sure you brush your teeth afterwards." So, I think to myself, what does *that* mean? Anyway, I go to the bathroom and brush my teeth. And, I use *his* toothbrush too. It would've freaked him out if he knew; eggs on his toothbrush. So, later, he tackles me onto the bed, and I tell him I'm not interested, and he asks me, "What do you want *now*?" Like, three years ago, it was the exact same scene, only *then* he said, "What do you want?"

And *this* time he says, "What do you want *now*?" This guy is not a very good conversationalist, you know what I mean? So, I say, "You want me to say that I want you deep inside of me, don't you?" So, for a joke I tell him I'd fuck him for his birthday which is in three weeks. So, he's been extra nice to me, smiles a lot, even invited me to his show at the Palace. But, the jerk at the door had the nerve to charge me a cover, I mean, I'm a musician too. You don't ask your fellow performers to pay to see you. You just want them out there with you. So, the whole night Matt's ignoring me even though I'm sitting right near the front, maybe because I've got a guy with me, but big deal, it's not like we're kissing or holding each other's crotches under the table or anything, and he even said he was going to dedicate a song to me, but he didn't want to embarrass me, and I asked him who it was that he was *really* afraid of embarrassing. Anyway, so I introduce him to my friend, and I ask him why he ignored me all night, and then in the last minute he sits down at the table and starts talking to me. Like, did he think I was going to go home with him instead of my friend? But at least Matt introduced me to Rico, the jerk who works the door, which is a joke because we've known each other for years, we're all musicians, but at least now the door guy could see that I knew Matt, and so I tell Rico that next time I'd buy him a drink, but he better not ask me to pay cover again. So, Rico kisses me good night on the cheek. What a creep. He takes my money and then acts like such a close friend.

During Sarah's torrent of words, I gazed through the window at the sidewalk in front of the house. I thought of the Palace, a premium dive bar in the Annex district on Bloor Street. Two floors, with new music, alt-rock, punk rock, indie, sometimes goth. The outside decorated with bizarre caricatures painted in grotesquely bright hard-line colours. It used to be a silent-movie theatre back around 1910, redesigned by someone named Howard Crane who was based in Detroit. The first movie they showed was Cecil B. DeMille's *Don't Change Your Husband*, starring Gloria Swanson playing a woman who divorces her slob of a husband, and then marries another man, only to discover that he's a beast. After the divorce, her first husband improves his ways, and she realizes that he still loves her. She knows she's made a mistake, divorces the second husband and goes back to the first. The Palace. In 1980, the property got picked up by Chung Su Lee, a local Korean merchant who owned the Stop and Go corner store at Bathurst and Harbord. He turned the movie theatre into the Palace nightclub, much in the same spirit as the Cameron House in the Queen Street West artist's district. Mostly alt-rock at Lee's Palace. Dancing on the top floor. Live music on the main floor. Good acoustics. They've featured some big-name groups there: Bare Naked Ladies, Red Hot Chili Peppers, Smashing Pumpkins, Arctic Monkees, Nirvana, the Magnetic Fields, Our Lady Peace, Tragically Hip. Sarah's river of words kept flowing. I looked for Jesus on the sidewalk in front of my house, but he wasn't there. So, I turned back to the telephone.

'You know, none of this would've happened if my marriage had worked out. Matt is so strange. He likes lemon meringue pie, which I hate, so I thought I'd bring one over for his birthday, but then I thought, why should I? He doesn't care about me, and the only reason he's been nice to me is because he didn't get my joke about screwing him for his birthday. So, as we're leaving the Palace he asks me if I'm going to bring him a lemon meringue pie for his birthday, but I can see in his eyes he's got something else on his mind, so I tell him, "I'll bring you a lemon meringue pie when you make me an omelette." So later, I'm at the Cameron pub, and there's this guy there. He's kind of a fan of mine, always comes to my gigs, but he's broke and kind of sad, so I buy the guy a beer, and I tell him, "So long as I'm here, you got at least one friend in the room." So then, he wants to come home with me, and get me to make him to dinner, and he asks me if he can crash at my place, and he wants me to lend him fifty dollars, so I tell him to take a hike, and he says, "but I thought we were *friends*."

I'm always trying to help people, but it always backfires, you know? And there was this chick down the hall, she's moved out now, but she borrowed fifteen bucks, and then she used the money to buy a picture of this Bengal tiger she got at the Salvation Army store, you know? And then she tries to impress me with it. I mean, I thought she needed the money for food, or Tampax, or some shoes or something. And she asks me over to her place, and there's this strange guy visiting who thinks he's the Buddha or something, and he's on his knees in front of me. He had to be on s*omething*, and he says he loves me, and he hugs me with his face at my crotch, and I get pissed off and tell him to get away from me, and he says, "You act as if I've never been between your legs, but we were lovers in a previous lifetime." And he says that if anybody ever tries to hurt me, he'll kill them, and to prove it he grabs her cat and threatens it, and says, "I'll kill this cat for you!" But I say, "Don't kill the cat because if you do, how will you prove your love for me tomorrow?" So, he drops the cat and starts walking towards me on his knees, his arms outstretched with tears in his eyes, telling me how much he loves me. And in the meantime, when I'm not visiting, her boyfriend, not the space-case Buddha guy but *another* guy, keeps hanging around my place because he's bored when she's not home, and he expects me to make him tea or coffee every time, and so I make it for him. I don't know, I like helping people. So, I make him coffee, and then, this guy wants to borrow my guitar, or borrow my coffee table, and he wants to borrow twenty bucks, and then he wants to *keep* them. Like, what does he think I am, his fairy godmother or something? So, I say to myself, why am I doing this? I've got to stop letting people walk all over me. I mean, at first, I thought I'd be nice and helpful—really presumptuous of me, you know? Like a Mother Teresa complex or something, but then I realized that they just want to use me or use my stuff. They don't care about me. I'm just another twat with something they want, and these guys, they're all *Geminis*! Two-faced, you know. And they've all lost their jobs or money. It's got something to do with Gemini entering a new phase, and you know me, I'm a fool for Geminis, my husband was one. I really miss him, and I still cry about him sometimes, but he's gone now, and Matt's a Gemini, and so are those other two idiots, probably, I don't know. I'm like a magnet to them. It's got something to do with the moon. They're all into a new cycle which I guess is good, because they're going to make a new start, but what about *me*? Here I am trying to help other people, but they're lowlifes. Users, you know? I mean I'm trying to get ahead too. I'm a giver, but such a fool, and I'm really getting crazy over it. I don't know if I should kill myself or go to the laundromat. And, I've gained weight! Do I look overweight to you? Oh yeah, we're on the phone, never mind. And my feet are swollen, and my shoes feel too tight. I'm so neurotic, do you think I should do a show now, or wait until September when I'll really be ready? I'm afraid to get back on the stage again. I don't know why, but I'm afraid people will get jealous of me, or I might start crying onstage. Those songs that I wrote, they came from my heart, out of the blue, they mean something, a part of me that I didn't know existed, but I don't want to get mean or become an animal. I've got a strong Leo influence. I can be tough, but I don't want to be *too* tough. Am I too tough? Like, do you think I'm too much of a beast?'

So, I told her that I was of two minds, and on the one hand, she had to take care of herself, and maybe sometimes she *had* to be a beast. All she had to do was work with musicians and artists who were already making it, and then she'd find a new set of friends, leave all that crap behind, and it'd be like a fairy tale, even though fairy tales don't happen in real life. And she said, 'Do you really think so?' And I said, sure, one day she'd get a gig at the Palace, and have a ball, and maybe some talent scout would be in the audience, and she'd make it big-time, even if there are no happily-ever-afters in real life.

So, I told her about Selene, the Titan goddess of the moon, who fell in love with Endymion. Selene was the daughter of the Titans Hyperion and Theia. Selene's sister was Eos, goddess of the dawn, and her brother was the sun god, Helios. She had several lovers, including Zeus, Pan and Endymion. She's also known as Luna. And like her brother Helios, who rides his sun chariot across the sky each day, Selene rides her moon chariot across the heavens each night. I told Sarah that Endymion was the first mortal to follow the movements of the moon, and so he fell in love with her. It's said that with Endymion, Selene had fifty daughters, who represent the fifty lunar months of the Olympiad. She thought Endymion to be so beautiful that she asked Zeus to grant him eternal youth so that he would never age or die or leave her. Zeus agreed, but only on condition that Endymion would sleep and dream eternally. And so, Endymion dreamt forever in a cave on Mount Latmus. And, Selene came each night to gaze at her beautiful sleeping lover.

Sarah thought about that for a moment, and said she hadn't met any Endymions. 'But hope springs eternal, and maybe someday, someone will wake up and notice me.' And she said that she'd been deserted so many times, that she was thinking of changing her name from Sarah to Sahara. And I told Sarah that maybe she was going through a kind of trial by fire. 'If you're cleaning the inglenook, then you're going to get covered in ashes, and you might even get burnt, but it's part of a process of self-actualization, a cycle, a transformation, ashes to ashes.' She paused, and said, 'Inglenooks are beautiful, especially with a good fire going. I studied Frank Lloyd Wright at art college, so I've seen some great designs. But, all that ashes-to-ashes stuff, I don't know.' And I said, 'Even though she began by sweeping ashes, Cinderella was a kind of Bodhisattva because she rose above it all.' And Sarah said, 'I'm not sure about that Eastern stuff. I'm Jewish, you know.' And I wanted to tell her about Abraham; when he spoke to God, he felt humbled because he knew he was nothing more than dust and ashes. And I wanted to tell her my dream about Jesus. And I wanted to tell her how it's mindfulness, and not matter that's at the heart of being. But then I was of two minds on that, because, where is your heart when you're unconscious like Endymion? And I wanted to tell her how possibility arises from the individual, but first there's separation, and solitude, and suffering, but I figured she probably already knew that. So, instead, I said, 'You're a fire sign, right? Maybe you need a water sign, for balance. Anyway, you're just waiting for a new *dawn*, and *one* day, your prince will come.' And she said, 'I never knew anyone named Don, but I know that Matt wants to come on his birthday. And that Don guy better not be a Gemini!'

So, I told her about an article I read in the newspaper. There was this armoured truck from Loomis, and one of the three guards in the truck had scribbled a note and shoved it in the window. And the note said, 'Help, I'm being held hostage.' A passing motorist noticed the sign and reported it to the police. Next thing you know there's a city wide dragnet. Police were driving around, looking for anything big and grey and moving. They had cruisers search all over Metro. The provincial police joined the hunt. Meanwhile, the truck was already fifteen minutes late for its next stop. The police tracked an armoured vehicle north of the city near Bathurst and Highway 7, but it was a Brink's truck, not a Loomis. The cops checked the route where the Loomis truck normally stopped, including the pizza joint where they usually had lunch. They finally caught up with it in the northwest part of the city around Weston Road near Sheppard. The two guards came out with their hands up when they saw the police cruiser pull them over, but the driver locked himself inside until officials from the company showed up about half an hour later. The guards and driver were all in their mid-twenties. Just average guys, with names like Dick and Bob, the kind you might remember skipping classes with at high school, so that you could shoot a few rounds of pool, maybe have a drink and a smoke. Later, they were all charged with public mischief.

And so, Sarah asked me what all this had to do with her. So, I said, 'Look, let's say you're inside one of those armoured trucks. And you sometimes imagine what it would be like to have all that money or gold, and you think about what you would do with it all, even though you realize that you wouldn't likely get your hands on that kind of money, not in a million years.' But she interrupted me before I could finish, and said, 'Yeah, that reminds me of this woman I know, she's always talking about Bob Dylan, and how she was Bob Dylan's girlfriend for a while, and all I wanted to know was, how was he in bed, but she told me it wasn't any of my business. People are always telling me what is and isn't my business. She was always talking about the weird head-trips he was on and all that, and I said, so what? It's nothing that you wouldn't read about in *Rock Express*, and it seemed to me she was always exaggerating. And anyway, I never wanted to know if he was a prince, just if he was any good in bed.'

So, I said, 'Well, that's one prince who could easily get a gig at the Palace.' And, I wanted to say something about how trapped we get, especially when we're locked-in on sex or money. So, I got back to the armoured car incident and told her how they called it the 'Looney Tunes' chase, because it was in pursuit of something crazy. And I explained that the story was related to another situation that happened a while earlier when the back door of a different armoured vehicle suddenly burst open. This kind of thing happens from time to time. It happened in Toronto along the Gardiner Expressway. And it happened on Interstate 20 in Weatherford, Texas. And it's always a big pile of money. The truck's backdraft sucks hundreds of thousands of dollars out the back door. And motorists go loony, stop their cars and cause traffic jams while money floats up and down the freeway in the northbound and southbound lanes, cross streets, east and west. People get out of their cars, grab up as many bills as they can, stuff them into their pockets. One news agency reported money flying everywhere. People grabbed fistfuls. Another report said it looked like an Easter egg hunt. People bent over grabbing as much as they could, and then they jumped back into their cars and drove off. The armoured-car company is still waiting for the return of hundreds of thousands of dollars. They put ads in newspapers saying things like, 'If you picked up any money on the expressway, we'd appreciate its return. Your identity will be protected, and you won't be charged with theft.' The ads ran for about a month, so you can guess what kind of a response they got. 'Thank you, sir, for returning this twenty-thousand-dollar bundle, you are a gentleman, allow me to give you a firm handshake.' So, I explained to Sarah that life's a double-edged sword, and everyone gets lucky *once* in a while.

Sometimes stuff just happens. But other times, we believe we want something, even if it's not what we need. And so, she said, 'I think I see what you mean, but I don't want to end up like some rock-and-roll Cinderella, talking about it in some dive bar after midnight when the carriage and horses have disappeared, and I'm back on the streets again.' And she said, 'Thanks for telling me all that. I guess I'll do the laundry now.' And she hung up.

Following her phone call and my lost dream, I grew listless within the confines of the house and decided to take a walk. I headed south on the sidewalk, looking for something, something different, but was met only by a blue-sky day, tall oak branches shifting in the west wind and an empty street. I couldn't return to my dream, so I began to think of what Endymion might recall if he awakened on the side of Mount Latmus, what dreams he might share atop the breakneck stone spurs of that steep mountainside. Latmus rests in the Muğla province of Turkey and is part of the Beşparmak range formed through a collision of tectonic plates. The massif rises along the north shore of the Latmian Gulf, tackled by clouds kneeling to sunset as the glowing nets of fishermen close each day. The Gulf opens to the Aegean Sea but is fed by the sweet waters of the river Maeander. At dusk, Selene rises past the Temple of Athena on her ascent into the wolf-howl night, accompanied by silent owls in flight, rising above sleeping beasts enfolded in the tumbling woods. Having walked south for over a city block, I realized that I had seen nothing. So, I turned about, and returned to the house. I felt an idiot joy as a warm breeze arose behind my back, carrying me home.

WATCH, WATCHING

Now, the warm autumn rains have begun, and yellow leaves sweep about my feet as I walk to work. Lately, she's been sending me links to kink pages. Research for a new book. Leather-bound, corsets, harnesses, halters, for her or him, latex and PVC, all tastefully illustrated with attractive models: busty, long-legged women, lean, muscular men. Toying with mischief. Enticing, the way it was that summer night. Yesterday, it was nurse and doctor outfits, naughty patient gowns. Stockings, hose and thigh-high fishnets, vintage style replicas of the '40s with the back seam, garter belts and naughty illustrations from the days after the Second World War. Eisenhower vintage. She sends them to my work email, which I find mildly embarrassing but secretly stimulating. Restraints, braces, dungeons in a box, all shipping details accompanied by friendly-looking receptionists—actually, actors or actresses in costume, players playing, purportedly ready to respond immediately to your phone call or Internet order. Adult services. I flip to other emails, try to be discreet when my secretary walks in to bring documents for signature. Or, I forward the messages accompanied with her coy comments to my private email where I can consider them and the websites later, in greater leisure and privacy. I recall that midsummer night. She said, 'Just because we're going to your place for a drink doesn't mean anything will happen.' I agreed, and had no reason to think otherwise but was intrigued. We talked politics, poetics, drank wine. I've moved since then, to another house. My short-term lease was up in the summer home. I had hoped to find something more permanent by summer's end. Instead, I now find myself bouncing from place to place. Nomadic. In transition. Searching. It was only a couple of days after the encounter when I received an electronic message:

Lost: Bangle-style with simple face, contemporary ladies' watch. Open links on either side of face and smaller links on underside. Adjustable. Face, mother-of-pearl accented with gold hands and markers complementing polished gold-tone case and bracelet. Scratch-resistant crystal. Water resistant to 30 metres. Jewellery-style clasp. Sentimental value. Reward if found.

I remember the moment. Her sudden decision to take it off. The abandon, and the relief. 'I'm taking this watch off. Hmph.' I can situate myself in that moment. I am there, near her, watching her hand place it on a nearby ledge. I seem to remember a ledge above my head at the time. But I could be wrong. I was—we were—intoxicated, by each other, wine, poetics, casting a net of words arcing from Yeats to Olson, a wide net stretching from the early myths to Graves counting the slow heartbeats and the bleeding-to-death of time, Eliot and what the thunder said, and Edward Lear, the blues, the Beats, the Roxy Music of passion, dissonance, the moan of doves in immemorial elms, even Tennyson, when the blood creeps and the nerves prick, when time is a maniac scattering dust, or life a fury slinging flame, and we spoke of Bishop's September rain and what we planned when summer changed to autumn with the iron kettle singing on the stove, and Stein's roses, and Stein's roses. The art of Picasso, Cubist constructions, and his African influence. The night was hot, and words steamed around epics, vengeful gods, mornings after, the *jouissance* of Handel's royal fireworks, Huxley and his doors of perception lighting our fires. Diviners and divinations. I-Ching, Tarot, and what the cards said. At one point, half-attentively, I watched her open the clasp and thrust her watch on a ledge. The ledge seemed higher at the time, but perhaps I only thought that because I was not standing. I can't remember precisely, but I think I was lying down, but near. Her. I can't remember exactly when the watch came off. We were talking, sitting on the couch, drinking French Syrah. Talking books, periodicals. Cards on the table. At some point, we kissed. I am there now, in thought, and it is earlier, perhaps later, or both, and we are standing at the fridge pouring wine into glasses. Talking dreams, and she's telling me that I'm talking to her head, not her body, taking her seriously, radical poetics, muses and writings. We draw arcs of thought in the midnight air, and she digs that I'm talking to her head; it arouses her, in her loins, she says, and she likes the wine. Debating metaphor as opposed to accumulation. Bodies. Tongues in motion. An undefined time later, was it back at the couch, my head resting on her breast? Breathing thick, warm breath, arousing. Was it at the fridge that she took off the watch? Tossed it on top, maybe? Or by the couch, at the window ledge. What did she say? 'I don't want to wear this right now.' Or was it 'anymore'. 'I'm taking it off. Umphff.' She pulled it off with joyful abandon. I remember remarking on it. In my thoughts. Momentarily considering how released she seemed, the watch unclasped. Off. I remember thinking how perhaps I should move it somewhere where it could be found easier later, but also thinking how the ledge, or wherever it was seemed a perfectly safe place, and how I shouldn't interfere with people's actions, how, if she liked it there, wanted to leave it there, it was all right. Let it be. A couple days later, the email. In cryptic fashion, phrased like a want-ad for the newspaper, discreetly seeking a lost item. Promising a reward to an audience of one. The form of the email, an inside joke, made me laugh. But the reward part grabbed me. What exactly would be the currency of thanks? Leather or rubber accessories, gloves, boots, bodysuits, the vengeance of the furies, or graces of the triple moon goddess? I scanned the other emails she sent as well. Her 'lost' electronic message arrived at my office mid-morning. I wanted to go to the house right away and start looking. Wanted to throw off the office, leave it behind. Release myself. She said, 'Just because we're doing this doesn't mean I'm leaving him.' And of course, I agreed. Transitions. Intersections. Ships passing on a midsummer's night. A cliché perhaps. Still, there was the matter of the lost timepiece. Lost in a moment when neither of us was fully attentive. Sucked down some warp-hole or lying near the crumbling flanks of a half-formed memory. She got that watch from her erstwhile lover. Perhaps there was to be more with him. She hoped or meant for more, but somehow ... time. Searching, I was conscious of the importance of not creating a fiction of what had happened, conscious of the importance of not re-creating the moment, for in that re-creation there was bound to be distortion. Conscious of the need to suspend what I thought had happened and instead simply search without preconceptions as to the location of the thing. I knew if I projected onto memory, then it would metamorphose into a self-wrought story. The preconceived layers of events re-created would blur the actual. I had to suspend, stop time. Thought. Wait for a period. At home. I searched the obvious places. Top of the fridge, window ledge near the couch, surrounding areas, between cushions on the couch, then the floor. The obvious places. I tried to suspend any internal dialogue, tried to see, remember what was there then, on the night of.

Searched the second floor, bedrooms, closets, memory and slippage. Again, the window ledge, sheets, pillows, slipcovers, behind the couch in case it slid there, under, or onto the carpet. Blurs, slippage, new thoughts bumping into memories of the actual. Recalling motion, the porch, the slow dance of actions. Inside the house that night, she, wanting. Wanting me, inside. Aroused, drunk, outside of our heads, beyond the world's sticky grasp. Thinking hard. Mother-of-pearl. Smaller links. Spent. Her face in morning, obscured by locks, links of hair, pale features, sun, gold, the face clasped, calm, accented with open hands, nose almost aquiline, cool morning shadows accentuating cheekbones, lips, drawn, dawn, a photograph, discreetly sunlit through dim clouds, the city awakening, morning, a portrait, a series of photos stored in flawed memory, thinking of Stevens's blackbird, and his thirteen ways of looking as I flip through moments layered, watching, seeking a watch that cannot be found. I could see, really see inside her, the distanced beauty, and when I spoke of it, she brushed me off with mock derision, then asked for more. Skin, supple, heart turning its gaze upon itself, deep gaze into, what was it? Later, she said, 'Just because I misplaced that watch doesn't mean ...' Twelve years. Her time. But no commitment. Nothing ventured. Years lost, perhaps, but nothing truly lost ... except. She, thinking maybe marriage, with him, or another. And then this, what? Passage or digression? And of all times, at solstice. Diametrically opposed to the halcyon days of winter. A magic equilibrium. A match struck. Eyes illuminated by the candle's flickering. Fingering. Books. Each other. Traces. Beautiful losers. Something gained, maybe. Me, thinking God is alive, Nietzsche is dead, buried by latex kink fetish nurses in a freshly turned plot. 'I'm not really into the heavy bondage,' she says. 'But sometimes, I like the aesthetic.' Research. And I'm listening, drinking her words with red wine.

And now, me, revisiting moments in time, unclasping temporal pockets that insisted themselves during the night when words gave shape to fists raised previously in passion with smashed glasses, missed appointments, opportunities. Her closeted places, momentarily unlocked to reveal a coterie, half forgotten. I listened, parched, perched, awaiting flight, restrained and bound, awaiting release, a caged bird, singing words, a command or permission, or ships, anchored adjacent on the wine sea that brought us together. At port. No fixed destination. Me departing marriage. After twelve years. She considering one. Or not, the unspoken thought. Uncovering old sores, the bitter taste of each other's pasts, inventing winter futures. Wine coaxing, tongue fury, eyes on hands, loosened clothes, but still of two, maybe, three minds. Tongues freed, falling into each other's orbits, mouths, bodies. Later, the morning. Then, a couple days later, the email: 'lost watch' and me searching mind and house, passing through that night again, bits at a time. Not knowing which to prefer, the beauty of inflection or the beauty of innuendo. I was relishing the pleasant anxiety of the task. But left wanting. 'He gave me that watch.' Thinking perhaps the loss or absence might somehow signify something of import. Innuendo. Sentimental value. An undefined inflection. The need to be on time for work, meetings, buses. Timing, a real need. And, now, me searching, and while searching, re-tracing our steps, movements. Hot breath on neck. Biting. Gentle. Or gentle-hard. Or hard. Her mouth, and mine. Wine and words. Touching. Crazy with night. We spoke paths. Opposite trajectories. But for the passing. Dancing. Predestination or free will. Veering. Comets accelerate when hurtling too close to planetary or stellar gravitational fields. 'I'll never leave him.'—'Of course.' And we both knew. And it was at this pocket of time, a closet where we hang umbrellas or coats, where we hesitated, came to a momentary standstill. I remember, here, time, breath, stopped for a period. It is little, but perhaps little enough, or more than enough. Thinking, there sometimes comes a moment when you hesitate, and say this isn't right, better withdraw, simplify, surrender to the confinement of words, and the lonely clasp of talk alone. But there also comes a time when someone says, there can only be a single moment, brief as it is, in which passion rises, and on passing is gone forever, without return. And caution can't help. It needs to be fed or it will consume you instead, and to give in to caution, or to refuse to unlock the clasp is bondage, is to capitulate to the condition of absence unendurable, and to condone a hunger that renders the spirit too weak to sing for its breakfast. Abstinence and denial collide with tongue and thigh. Inflected innuendo arrested. Sometimes you must make the wrong choice, or you're dead, and you stay that way and know it. Sometimes it's best to leap without a parachute, into free-fall, to land on a couch, or a bed, taste hot summer in your mouth. Amidst the thunder and words, her aestive carnality reigned that night. And later, I found myself musing, recalling all this while searching for a timepiece. Thinking, maybe she still has it, always had it, but wants me to look, look back. An arch dig, a playful card, knowing that as I'm looking, I'll be re-tracing the steps, here where we embraced, here, when we first touched glasses brimful with red wine, tracing, was it here, on the couch where we talked for, what was it? Hours or seconds? Later, stars, the stairs, a room and the window with ledges, a bed where madness met delirium in the intoxicated night and sleep emerged as victor, where morning fingered her hair, her quiet shoulder, where dawn touched our lips awake. And so, I'm watching, searching, looking for a watch, but not finding it. Wandering, bemused, wondering, if maybe she still has it because I can't find it, or if she took it without thinking, or perhaps it will yet return or be returned, or one day be found in the bottom of a bag or drawer. And I'm thinking, perhaps the plumber, or electrician, or one of the maintenance people saw it, a day or so later. So many comings and goings, preparing the house, repairing it after my reasoned complaints to the landlord; minor matters. The overhead light switch broken. The leaking tap. Broken locks on the window. Perhaps one of them noted the watch on the ledge, and without thinking put it safely aside, perhaps in one of my many cluttered drawers, or thinking swiftly, seized the purloined moment and stuffed it into a pocket. Our haste that morning did not enhance reflection, departing without breakfast. I'd gladly purchase a replacement. But there is the other matter of sentiment buried under temporal inflection, perhaps too personal an innuendo. Or, perhaps it will return at an unexpected moment stimulated by some liminal event, a tune on the radio, the turning of a card, or a page, and as I search the house, I pause momentarily at the inescapable rhythms of sleeping breath, rumpled sheets, morning, a sea washing through the window's glass, looking to the ledge for a watch that might've been there, is not there now, but if it was eyed and found, clasped in hand, passed to a second hand in an unbound moment, then time would stop.

THE FRESHNESS
OF A DREAM

My mother and I are sitting at her kitchen table. She sits with her back to a glass storm door. I gaze at the tangled garden behind her. My mother is quietly crocheting a hat for my son. She peers through her glasses. Her old fingers nimbly turn the wool strands on light metal crochet hooks. It's time for another tea, but I'm held in place by a strange inertia. To break the inertia, I ask her what happened to her brother during the war, my uncle Joe. She fed me small pieces of that story before, but I hunger for more.

My uncle had been fighting with the partisans, first against the Nazis, then the Soviets. My mother informed me that he was tossed into a mass grave, only to be retrieved. The entire nation had been forcibly 'occupied'. The bulldozer driver, a patriot, was ordered by a Soviet commander to cover up dozens of bodies. The bulldozer driver refused. He'd witnessed several fingers moving on my uncle's left hand. They threatened to kill the 'dozer driver. He rejected their threat. 'I'm the only bulldozer driver for hundreds of kilometres. If you kill me, you'll have mass contagion.' The commander shrugged, relented, but remained pissed off. He ordered a pair of soldiers to haul my uncle's body out of the trench. The 'dozer driver ensured they hospitalized him. I'm told that my uncle was among several partisans sitting in the back of a resistance truck, the kind with a canvas tarpaulin covering the back. The truck driver inadvertently trundled up to an unexpected military checkpoint. Realizing the danger, the driver stomped on the gas, swerved past the checkpoint barrier, but one of the ground troops managed to lob a grenade. My uncle was near the front of the truck-bed. Knocked unconscious, he was bloodied, blinded, and crippled on his right side. The bodies of the other partisans shielded him. I wanted to know more. My mother kept crocheting. 'Tell me more about what happened to Uncle Joe.' This fall it's been unseasonably warm. A reprieve.

Sun dances lightly on shifting shadows beneath the backyard maple. I watch yellow leaves swirl across the lawn. There is a light breeze, and I really should be outside raking. But it is so comfortable in this kitchen and I don't want to miss what she will say when the spirit moves her. 'Today is the first of the month. She tells me, 'October is *veļu mēnesis*, the spirit moon, the time when they return among us.' I nod and sip my lukewarm tea. 'If you like, I'll read your cards.' I nod again. She puts down the crocheting and clears the table. I think today we should light a candle. She hands me the cards. The cards are from a regular deck, all four suits from nines up to aces. 'Shuffle the deck and think about what was behind you.' I've had these readings since boyhood. They always start the same way and are almost always right. It's uncanny but I no longer question it. When I was younger, I thought she was eavesdropping on my conversations over the phone, or learning of my activities some other way, and, as a devoted mother, was using the readings to warn me of my own stupidity. It drove me crazy. I surreptitiously hid magazines under the mattress, foolishly forgetting that she was the one who usually changed the sheets. Now, she's old, lame in one leg, her one good ear is almost deaf. I have to find the right frequencies when I speak, so that her hearing aid picks up my words. I know she can't overhear any of my conversations, so I reason there must be something else to her card readings. I let her do the talking. The hearing aid never seems to work correctly, but I've learned that silence and simple gestures work as well as words. She lights the candle and we begin. 'Now cut the cards three times towards yourself.' I know this without her saying it, but sometimes she uses a different approach, so I quietly follow directions. She observes the cards in three piles and says, 'It's good. You are no longer dwelling on the past, but there is an open space before you. You don't know what to do yet. Give it time.' We begin. She starts laying out cards on the table.

I remember the day she told me about how she learned this divination ritual. I was only half paying attention, mildly intrigued and slightly bored during that ordinary summer day. I remember her words, about how it was back in the old country, on the farm they used to have. 'Gypsies', Roma people coming from the south, would visit them in Daugavpils en route to Riga. There were so many stories about those strange visitors. Daugavpils, sometimes called Dvinsk, is near the Russian, Polish and Lithuanian borders. Her neighbourhood was mostly Roman Catholic and Jewish. Earlier during the war, the Nazis rounded up the Jews, and my mother visited her former neighbours in the prison camp. It was dangerous. Had the guards known she was bringing food they would've shot her. A blithe smiling girl of fifteen smuggling dark rye bread and other goods in her school bag. She was 'just visiting.' They indulged her. What could such a young girl do? Sometimes they questioned her on the way out. 'What did you talk about?' 'Not much, the weather, how long they've been here. How long they might have to wait before they get out.' She knew the right answers.

Now, sitting in my mother's kitchen, I think back on those times. 'Shuffle the deck again and concentrate on what is in your heart.' I am shuffling and staring blankly at the sun-dappled yard beyond my mother's shoulder. When the war broke out many fled. My mother's family's farmhouse was a yellow-brick two-storey with a pair of fireplace chimneys rising above a terra-cotta roof. Their little farm was near the town. Next to their home was a small schoolhouse that my grandfather managed. He was the principal. For my mother, school was not a priority. But, she did well, and following high school graduated from the School of Commerce just as war began dismantling their lives. Now, she's telling me that before things turned sour, one sunny Saturday afternoon, a band of Roma people rolled onto the farm-stead, uninvited. The locals called them 'čigāni.' It was late summer. The čigāni had two brown horses, each drawing a tar-paulin-covered wagon, en route to the marketplace in Riga. They had found ways to make themselves tolerable, even wel-come. They brought small items to trade: semi-precious jew-ellery, dolls, toys, silk cloths, perfumes, scarves, hats, and such. And music. They made music with a worn violin, cymbals, an accordion, flutes, and a tambourine. They were tinkers and could quickly repair pots or pans. Their matriarch read cards. The farm folks granted them a welcome, and they politely entered the house. Tea was offered to all. Tea—or 'chai' as it was called—was a social obligation. The family kept a large samovar, and they fed fresh tea and water into it all day long, sometimes for several days in a row. Potent stuff. Grandfather sat with the bunch of them chatting and drinking chai. After a while, the matriarch wandered over to the kitchen, and stood there observing my grandmother preparing a large pot of por-ridge. At the time, my mother's four brothers were outside doing chores. They're all dead now. All older. All dead. The two youngest were twins. The matriarch approached the stove, 'Please mistress, some porridge for my family?' My grandmother did her best to ignore her and kept stirring the pot. 'Some porridge for my children?' My grandmother looked the old woman in the eye. 'Children? They're adults and perfectly capable of caring for themselves. Hardly children. We'll be serving supper when the cows come in. This oatmeal is for the cowherds. The rest of us will get our dinner soon enough.' She kept stirring. 'Please missus, we've travelled far and we're hungry.' She held out her cupped hands. My grandmother, fed up with the old woman's wheedling, lost her patience. 'Fine, here, have some!' My mother's mother withdrew a large wooden spoon from the pot and swiftly dolloped a wad of hot oatmeal into the old woman's hands. That's when she learned why it's best to humour Roma, to humour čigāni, even when they pester you. The woman shouted, 'It's hot! Hot!' She quickly rolled the porridge back and forth from right hand to left, noisily spat onto it, and hurled it back into the pot. Grandmother shrieked. 'Ahh! You've ruined it! You *spit* onto it! Ach. What have you done! *Šausmas!* Horrors! Oy! Here ... you might as well take the pot. I'll start another, and *no more tricks!*' The Roma knew that welcomes were rare and repaid my grandmother's reluctant kindness with several card readings, token gifts, simple magic tricks and music. Soon, the Roma would be forced into death camps along with Jews, Catholics and other religious groups including Jehovah's Witnesses, as well as beggars, the homeless, political dissidents, the disabled and anyone who didn't conform to Nazi expectations of gender or sexuality. My mother, still a young girl, watched as the old Roma woman read cards for the family. With my mother watching by her side, the old woman explained card divination. My mother never forgot.

It's October now, and my mother has spread my cards on the table. She has read my cards many times. I remember her recent divinations. 'There are long journeys to come. They end well.

Someone says, you are spending a disproportionate time on details that don't matter. What does "disproportionate" mean? I never use that word.' Sometimes when reading cards my mother would channel. Her eyes would close, and she'd begin each sentence with, 'Someone says ...' In my youth, I thought she was faking, but I soon realized that the words she used were outside her vocabulary.

I remember what she told me about the Roma visit and how her youngest brother decided to play some tricks. While the Roma and Grandfather were inside drinking chai, my uncle enlisted a couple of farmhands, and along with his brothers, used a rope and pulley to haul one of the wagons up a ramp into the barn rafters. Then, he got a bucket of whitewash, and painted large white daubs onto the two Roma horses. Later that day, as the čigāni were preparing to leave, the patriarch nearly lost his mind. 'My horses! My wagon! They've been stolen!' The four brothers had a big laugh about this and asked him to look again. 'The pasture has a fence. Your horses couldn't have escaped!' The Roma elder squinted at several dappled horses calmly grazing in the field. 'But I *have* looked and none of those horses are mine!' My grandparents weren't in on the joke and didn't understand. This added to the prank's effect. Later, my mother's brother revealed all. My grandmother scolded the boys. 'Don't laugh at their misery! God's punishment comes to us all! Remember, it was čigāni who stole the nails that were intended to crucify Jesus!' This sobered them up. They had all heard the story of how a Roma nail-smith was ordered by a Roman legionnaire to make a dozen nails and upon learning their purpose, bid his son to run away with three of them, so that he could say he hadn't time to finish the work and perhaps they would delay the crucifixion. Somewhat abashed, my uncle Joseph confessed that the pranks were his idea. Instead of being angry, the Roma laughed and jokingly slapped him on the back.

My mother's hands and voice are always steady when she turns the cards. She typically says things like, 'Good news from a short road. In the evening hour. You will hear it, maybe on telephone or email. A nice couple will invite you somewhere. Go. It is good for you to be out. Now is a good time to be talking to people.' She pauses often, speaks in broken sentences. But, when her eyes are half-closed, her voice takes on a different cadence, and a different voice speaks. 'Use your time wisely. Don't get drawn into arguments. Keep your cool. Someone says, "Be pragmatic about your choices."' And then, 'What does pragmatic mean? I never use such words. What is pragmatic?'

Outside, sun dapples the leafy shadows in the backyard. It was almost this time of year when the Cuban missile crisis was happening. We were boys playing hockey on the back streets of Toronto. At that time, the Second World War was still fresh in people's minds. There was talk about Korea and Indochina. Vietnam. We were in Toronto's west end. They sounded air-raid sirens twice a day—once in the morning as we awoke and again in the afternoon not long before suppertime. War seemed imminent, inherent, inevitable.

At school they taught us about the DEW-Line, an early warning radar network. I had just turned ten. It was all over the news. A U-2 had taken photos of missile sites in Cuba. Our boyish minds couldn't quite grasp the meaning of mid-range ballistic missiles, but we understood about nuclear bombs. We had all watched Walter Cronkite's television show on the 20th century. It was sponsored by the Prudential Insurance Company, which used the Rock of Gibraltar as their logo. We'd seen footage of A-bombs exploding and knew about Nagasaki and Hiroshima. At school, they ran us through air-raid drills. Our fifth-grade teacher was a nervous red-haired woman who preferred to wear grey vests, tartan skirts and black penny loafers. She seemed perpetually stressed. We were told that the school's PA system would announce any nuclear attack. Normally, the PA was used to play the national anthem each morning. Our classmates closest to the windows had the task of lowering the blinds in the event of an air attack. Our teacher explained, 'That's to prevent broken glass from flying into the room.' After the window-aisle kids lowered the blinds, they were to take cover under their desks. We'd mercilessly tease them. 'You're going to die first!' They'd cry. Nobody wanted to sit in the window aisle. The rest of the class would practise the drill, hiding under desks, 'In case plaster falls from the ceiling.' Sometimes our teachers ushered us in long lines to the basement. We'd wait in the bowels of the school, near the dank boiler room, where everything was painted industrial grey or drab green. After suppers, we watched the crisis unfold on television. We remembered Khrushchev from two years earlier when he banged his shoe on the table at the United Nations. This was no joke. We read newspapers after our parents were done with them. My family subscribed to the *Toronto Star*. Some of the other families subscribed to the *Telegram*. The 'Star' and the 'Telly'. Each day, we compared notes in the schoolyard. By October 22, the United States security systems were on alert at DEFCON 3. Missile launch pads and MiG jets had been spotted in Cuba. North America was the target. Today, I wonder how little the situation has changed. In Ukraine, the situation is critical. North Korea is developing long-range nuclear rockets. The A-bomb is still with us. Threats loom daily and war prevails. Back then, we spent time conjecturing on which major city would get hit first. Washington seemed obvious, but Ottawa seemed less important. New York, Detroit, Chicago, Miami, even Los Angeles seemed fair game. We worried about Toronto. It was on October 24th that they spotted

Soviet ships en route to Cuba. We learned those ships had nuclear missiles aboard. The U.S. raised its defence to DEFCON 2, one step away from full mobilization. At school, they provided more details about the DEW-Line. If missiles were fired from the Soviet north, they'd arc across the polar cap, fly over Canada to targets in the United States. We considered this possibility. If they came across the North Pole, it seemed certain that they'd target Ottawa, then Toronto. At recess, we'd form strategies. 'I heard some families have bunkers, but we don't have one.' 'Us neither.' 'If there's a war, maybe we'll go to the basement, or the cottage and hold out there until it's over.' 'You jerk, if there's a war, we'll all be fried to a crisp by the bombs.' 'Not me, I'm hiding in the basement. My mom has fruit preserves and we'll have enough food for a month.'

The families on my street were mostly DPs. Displaced persons. None of our parents had much faith in the Russians, and the idea of war was still fresh in their minds. I was born in the fall. My birthday became an excuse for my parents to socialize, to bring a wide range of friends into our home. I remember balloons, cakes, cigarettes, and alcohol. At different times, my mother prepared food. I remember different buffets, some with poached salmon, shrimp, meat kabobs, herring in tomato sauce, other buffets had smoked eel, smoked salmon, mixed bean salads, Waldorf salad. Sometimes there were little buns stuffed with onion and bacon known as *pirags*, marinated herring, potato salad, devilled eggs, home-baked caraway-seed-topped buns (*ķimen rauši*), apple bread, or a raisin-saffron bread called 'klinger'. Occasionally, my mother went to the trouble of baking a homemade Black Forest cake. My father worked as a carpenter. My mother worked at a restaurant, but on the side worked as a caterer and never skimped when it came to food. Everybody would drink beer, or whisky with ginger ale, or vodka straight, or wine, and sometimes all of these. Kids were allowed ginger ale or 7-Up which filled our noses with gas bubbles and tickled our throats. While our parents were drinking and yakking, we'd drag the only phone in the house into the hallway and make prank calls, dialling at random. 'Is your television on? How does it fit?' 'Is your refrigerator running? You better catch it—it just ran out your back door.' The air was filled with noise and cigarette smoke, while my cousins, my sister and I goofed off. For a while, everybody would argue about what happened in the last war and speculate on what was next. Then, the singing would start. They always sang in Latvian.

> Along the road back to the village
> Thoughts slip to rose-garden blooms
> With light footsteps, smiling faces
> Your childhood days do drift away,
> Greet the flowers, greet the sunshine
> A bird pronounces from a grove
> Friend, preserve your childhood dreams
> And save them deep within your heart.

Songs were how my people dealt with everything. For entries or exits from this world, for joy, or sorrow, for days lost or forgotten, for courage and endurance, for mocking enemies, for lusty passion, marriage or journey, there was always a song.

After such gatherings, there were half-empty bottles, and ashtrays filled with butts, and the following day in the school-yard, my small group of pals continued discussions about where to hide as the world teetered on the brink of nuclear war. We didn't grasp the full impact of the situation until the *Toronto Star* began carrying a series of editorial cartoons. We liked cartoons, but there was nothing funny about these. Each day the editorial featured a pen-and-ink drawing of a doomsday clock with the hour hand at high noon and the minute hand just seven minutes before the hour. The next day, the same cartoon appeared, the clock now set at six minutes to noon, with the grim reaper emerging from behind the clock. If the clock hit the hour, then we knew it meant nuclear war. In the classrooms, we kept practising safety drills and hiding under desks. I'd look up and see graffiti scribbled on the bottom of my desk, punctuated with a rainbow of gum wads. We knew we were going to die. Miraculously, Kennedy stood firm, and the missiles were returned to Russia. The crisis was averted, but in those days no one considered counselling for us kids, or even bothered to explain what had just passed. Classes continued as usual.

In my mother's garden, leaves flit over grass illuminated by warm sunshine. I shuffle the cards again, and without looking, randomly select from the deck until she tells me to stop. She spreads them on the table. 'You heard from an important man. Now, your troubles are behind you. It is good that you didn't rush into any business deals. You heard that somebody would lose a ring.' When she speaks like this, I understand that it is figurative. Another marriage breakup. I didn't need a fortune teller for that. My friends' lives are an open book. She keeps reading the cards.

I remember years ago, she always did the ironing on Thursday afternoons. I would read or do homework while she sang and worked. Songs cascaded one after the other. Back home, she sang in a choir. She had a lovely voice and sang her memories recalling old folk songs.

How years fly by,
swift as an agile swallow ...

It always seemed to rain on Thursday afternoons. Sometimes there was the roll of distant thunder as she slowly worked her way through the ironing. For no reason that I understood, I was moved to tears as I watched her, but I would hold them back, not wanting to upset her.

It is Thursday today and sitting together at this table is a little thing, but it is little enough. We are close to each other and I am at ease, listening to the words she gives me. The cards are on the table. Just last week she gave me these words: 'A surprising pleasant shock from a long road. You will hear of a man, a big shot. He is not well, but he is good for you. You are a little mixed up, not knowing which way to go, but it's okay. It will resolve itself soon, and then "boom". Everything will fall into place.' Swimming in an ocean of uncertainty, small comforts arise from knowing, or believing you know, what comes next.

It's times like this that I think back further, back to when we were small fry. My pal Wally and I would sit on the front lawn of his house, watching for the school bus. We'd watch in the mornings after breakfast. And we'd watch in the afternoons while munching Pink Elephant popcorn, the kind with a little prize inside. We treasured those prizes, and before we finished the popcorn we searched for a plastic-wrapped whistle, a miniature pair of dice, a tiny compass, or any small, hidden trinket. Wally's house stood opposite the school bus stop. We'd watch and speculate. A school bus would arrive. Brakes would squeal. The diesel engine belched noxious fumes. Children boarded, colourful in their September clothing. We never saw them return.

Perhaps certain thoughts came to mind because of our mixed Eastern European neighbourhood. At that time, Toronto's west end was mostly Polish and Ukrainian, with the odd

Lithuanian or Latvian family. Sometimes during evenings at home, our parents spoke in subdued voices about the Siberian Gulag. They spoke of prisons in the icy Taiga, where members of our families suffered excruciatingly prolonged deaths, even though the war had ended long ago. And, we heard about the horrors of concentration camps in Germany. Our families had lost members in both. We heard of the pogroms, and how people were taken away on trains but never returned. Our boyish minds made impossible leaps of logic. We didn't understand the concept of war, or school. Both were a mystery. An anxiety. Buses came and went. We watched, curious, anxious. Sometimes Wally's grandfather came out while we speculated on his front lawn. He was always trying to teach us a lesson. And he always made a point of shaking hands. He was missing the thumb on his right hand.

'You know how I lost this thumb? They *tortured* us. It was the *ghetto*. The *pogrom*! You boys ever heard of the Molotov-Ribbentrop pact?' When he started saying things like that, Wally's mother would yell at him in Polish. She'd shout through the front window telling him to stop. Wally's grandfather would shout back. 'My thumb is lost! People went missing! You want I should shut up? How are they supposed to know? Six million in one, twenty million in the other!' Later, we'd go inside. Eat chicken soup. Make plans. Other times, Wally came to my house. More soup. It was always soup and sandwiches for lunch. At night, my parents spoke of my father's brother. My uncle Peter. Imprisoned in Siberia. It was the late 1950s. He sent letters begging for food. We sent dry goods, rice, macaroni. The guards must've kept them for themselves. His letters never acknowledged our packets. At least by his letters we knew he was still alive.

On the streets, we ventured guesses about how life worked.

During evenings after school, we sat on the floor watching television. We learned what we could by watching TV. My parents regularly tuned into Cronkite's *The Twentieth Century* on CBS. Next day, during recess, we'd compare notes. I remember watching massive arrows arc across Europe, defining the trajectory of World War II. As kids, we were clueless. Dumbfounded, we watched footage of bombs dropping from warplanes, anti-aircraft guns strafing the night, concentration camps, human skeletons walking in striped uniforms.

Our lack of ease was fuelled by the air-raid sirens they tested each day. The sirens visibly rattled my mother as she prepared supper. In the afternoon, while we played outside, bombers traversed the sky. They flew from the Canadian Air Force Base at Downsview. Out-of-date green Shakletons, Lincolns and Lancasters conducted manoeuvres over the city. Their rumbling signalled their approach long before they arrived. War was fresh on everyone's mind. Everyone expected more war. We were ready. Wally and I and a few pals patrolled the street, took cover behind trees and garden fences, shot at those planes with wooden sticks and plastic rifles. For us, war was real, or, it was real enough.

When we were preschoolers our parents released us to the street each day. Back then, no one feared kidnappers or perverts. The street was ours so long as we looked both ways. I remember one particular time, reclining on Wally's front lawn. We were soaking up our last sun-filled summer of boyhood freedom, munching Pink Elephant popcorn, searching for tiny prizes, speculating on older children we'd seen taken away on school buses.

'They go, but I've never seen them come back ...'

'Yeah. I *knew* some of them.'

'What happens?'

'Don't know.'

Year after year, one after another, older brothers and sisters, our street friends, disappeared. We didn't know what happened. It seemed strange, foreboding. Unbeknownst to us, it was simple enough. Once enrolled, youngsters no longer roamed the streets with our gang. They sat all day in desks at school. Then, in the evenings, they were too tired to play, or were stuck doing homework. With those older kids gone, the street was ours. But soon, our time would come. So, during afternoons we sat on Wally's front lawn, speculating.

'Pretty soon, *we're* going to be on one of those buses.'

'Yup.'

'You think maybe they'll take us to one of those camps?'

'Maybe.'

'I don't want to go.'

'Me neither.'

We philosophized as only four-year-olds can, lolling on a lawn. We had no doubt that our heads contained all the worldly wisdom we needed. Looking back, I now realize that our boyish senses proved largely true in the years that followed. I recall that the Persian mathematician and poet Omar Khayyam once said that, when he was young, he eagerly frequented local doctors, mystics and saints to learn their wisdom on all things. But, one day, it dawned on him that each time he visited one of those sages, he'd exit the same door he'd entered. There was no sudden transformative illumination. Working with our God-given reason, we noted the fact that when the school bus doors opened, they swallowed up our comrades, but we never saw them return. Typically, our mothers called us back to our houses around 3:00 p.m. to wash up, do chores, get ready for supper. And so, Wally and I were always inside when the school buses returned. We never saw any of the older children come home. As far as we were concerned, it was a one-way trip.

The unspeakable consumed our minds. We were afraid to ask our parents. Immigrants. What would *they* know about school? Maybe they were somehow part of it. Anyway, school was for kids. This was *our* problem. We'd have to deal with it. We deliberated on cattle cars, deportations to death camps. The war was over, but we thought maybe this was how they did things nowadays. In Canada. Modern times. We speculated on what happened to survivors who might've fled. We heard rumours of older brothers and sisters who had returned. What had they done to regain freedom, home, and family? Seize a chance? Roll the dice? Take bearings on a compass to find their way home?

One September morning, around the time of my fifth birthday, I was marched off to kindergarten. It turned out that Wally was enrolled in a different school. Religious reasons. My mother dropped me off, placed me in the hands of a smiling teacher who towed me and several others into a large classroom. Trepidation gripped me. It was the largest room I'd ever seen, filled with strange smells and more children than I'd ever met, all in one place, at one time. The children there were already arranged in a large circle. There were two teachers in charge. Both wore long, plaid woollen skirts and starched white blouses. Those blouses demanded respect. My mother only wore such blouses on special occasions. For church, or funerals. The teachers were gentle but firm, ushering us to fill open spots in the circle. We waited nervously as others trickled in.

'What's going to happen?'

'Don't know.'

'Shh. They're looking at us!'

'Sit quietly, children. We'll begin soon. You'll have fun today.'

Their words calmed us, until we heard hysterical screaming in the hallway.

'Michael, behave! It's just school!'

The door to the hallway burst open, revealing a red-faced boy kicking, screaming, scrabbling away from the entrance. His mother's beehive hair-do collapsed as she and another teacher forcibly dragged him, one gripping a wrist and the other one of his ankles. His free leg dragged helplessly and he screamed constantly. As they dragged him through the portal we watched, horrified. He tore one hand free, clutched at the door jamb amidst horrible shrieks. It was chaos. Tears poured, unruly white shirttails hung loosely outside his trousers, his tie flew askew. His hair was wild, his black horn-rimmed glasses cock-eyed, nearly falling off. But his mother and the teacher prevailed.

'Look! He wears glasses, might be smart.'

'Maybe he knows something!'

'Let's get out of here!'

A small group of us rose to our feet, we surged toward the doorway. We figured if the teachers were busy with Michael, then we might have a chance. Better him than us. Or, maybe we could bail him out in the confusion. — We made a break for it, but the teacher's command froze us in place.

'Sit down this instant!'

Terrified, we halted, dead in our tracks. We were in for it now. Fingers pointed.

'Back to your places. Be seated, *immediately*, please!'

Trapped and shamefaced, we watched as Michael, still shrieking, was dragged to the circle. We glanced about nervously. At least we were still alive.

In those days, Toronto was called 'Muddy York'. At first, my parents lived on Lady York Street. Later, they moved to the west end, to the crest of the Humber River. Canada promised democracy, and back then our neighbourhood reflected at least some of those fundamental principles. Our public school had a broad mix of Irish, Scots, English, Eastern Europeans, and Japanese. Wealthy and poor.

I didn't know it at the time, but I later learned that I shared a classroom with children whose parents ran brokerages, law firms, tool and die factories, and major holdings like Maple Leaf Gardens. But the same classroom held kids whose parents were secretaries, furnace workers, waitresses, carpenters, taxi drivers, grocers, hairdressers, garbage-men, and construction workers. The parents on my street were from that second group. War refugees. DPs from the old world, out of place in the new. Skilled, but under-employed due to the language hurdle. Beyond our street we found ourselves amidst a broad mix of Catholics, Jews, Protestants, Anglicans and Greek Orthodox, all speaking different languages. It was Babel. Our refugee families were recent arrivals who hadn't fully grasped the basics of English. My father's broken sentences were thickly accented. For years he came home from work nearly in tears because they kept abusing him on the job. My mother was more adept. She worked as a translator for the British while escaping Europe. Meantime, the street kids I hung with spoke a haphazard English mixed with Polish, Ukrainian, Lithuanian, Yiddish and whatever else was spoken at home. We had our own lingo. As far as we were concerned, it was English. At home my family spoke Latvian. During afternoons and after street time, my mother taught me Russian. I resisted, demanded to know why I should learn that awful tongue. 'Always know the language of your enemy.' I didn't question that logic. But I never connected a face with the enemy.

After a week of kindergarten, I learned that we *were* permitted to return home each day. The bus picked me up in the morning and returned to my home street each afternoon. The bus ride reminded me of the parties my parents had at our house. Everybody sang on the way there and all the way back. We sang mindless standards: 'The Old Grey Mare', '99 Bottles of Beer on the Wall'. Our body heat caused the windows to fog up. We tried to attract the attention of people in nearby cars by drawing valentine hearts or swastikas on the windows. Our efforts were ignored. Some of us played X's and O's on the fogged-up glass. We soon learned that with a basic understanding the game was impossible to win. Thinking back, I pity the poor bus driver who endured our lack of social graces.

I remember one day, the kindergarten teachers stood us in a large circle and went around checking fingernails, teeth and shoes. I watched the two white blouses work their way around the circle. One kept record on a clipboard. As they drew closer, I listened carefully to how they spoke. It seemed another language. Not the street lingo we called English, and not what we spoke at home. Still, I comprehended. They wanted to know if we could tie our shoes. But the language seemed strange. I concluded that they spoke Russian.

The two blouses continued around the circle, and then, they stood before me. I held forth my nails, bared my teeth. They asked if I could tie my shoes. In Russian, I replied, 'Da.' They asked again. I repeated, 'Da. Da.' I was puzzled by their facial expressions. Looking back, I guess they thought that they were standing in front of a monosyllabic idiot. I was dismissed to the corner with the other social rejects. We stood in a cluster, consulting each other.

'What are you in for?'

'I took too long in the bathroom.'

'What about you?'

'Spilled paint during the art lesson. You?'

'They think I can't tie my shoes, but I *can*!'

The next day, I devised an alternate strategy. Again, the circle was formed. Again, they questioned everybody. When they came to me, I remained mute, smiled and pointed at my feet. I wore sandals. No laces. The teacher's complexion flushed. I could tell she was furious, but she remained strangely polite, demanding that I wear laced footwear the next day. Once again, I was relegated to the corner. Standing there in prison, a glimmer of understanding arose. At least for the time being, I was still alive.

———

Today, my mother looks at me from across the table. Beyond the glass door, afternoon shadows play through her tangled garden. The candle has shrunk a little. She hands me the cards. 'Now, shuffle and think of what's before you.'

UNDERSTANDING
THE SOUNDS YOU HEAR

For Nicole Brossard

'O God, I could be bounded in a nutshell and count myself
a king of infinite space, were it not that I have bad dreams.'
—*Hamlet*, Act 2, Scene 2

Valentine's Day has crept up without warning. Outside, it is
cold. Alone in my room, I have been rereading Shakespeare
and photocopying manuals for home appliances, because I must
leave, because I am broke and can live here no more. I received
a summons and must leave. I am photocopying manuals for
appliances because they will rent this place to someone else,
and the new tenant will want the old manuals for the appliances I have grown to love. It is peculiar perhaps, to grow to
love appliances, but when appliances are the source of nourish-
ment, and when they are there whenever one needs, standing as
a bulwark against the liquid vicissitudes of life, then, perhaps
'love' is not too extreme a word. Fond. 'Fond' is a worthy word.
But I feel more than fond. I have come to know these appliances. Personally. I will make copies of these manuals, page
after page. I must leave the appliances behind, but I will keep
duplicates of the manuals as a reminder. Duplicates. Like scrap-
books with pictures of old lovers. One day, my finances will
rally. I'll find new digs. I'll hunt through second-hand appliance
shops. I'll find identical, or near-identical appliances that I will
purchase for my own. It will be a kind of reunion with old

friends. In form, if not in fact. A reunion of sorts. And, I will have the manuals.

A summons was sent, and I must depart. Live elsewhere, with friends or family perhaps. Perhaps out of town. Elsewhere. Meantime, I glower at the makeshift sign indicating 'flat for rent' and, 'comes with appliances'. I am photocopying and drinking vodka that I keep ice-cold in the freezer. The viscosity of the vodka increases when refrigerated. It is cold outside, and as I awoke at morning's break, I recalled a dream. In the dream I was a prisoner. Guards interrogated me every day. Denied me water. Insisted I speak. It became repetitive. My name, my intentions toward authority, the real reason for my incarceration, any intelligence I might vend, proved pointless. Nothing I could say was deemed sufficient inducement to release me. I knew nothing and had nothing to say. Each day brought the same inquisition, the same litany of questions, always concluding with, 'What were you doing in the graveyard when we arrested you?' Bored, I soon responded to their questions with other queries, 'When churchyards yawn and hell itself breathes out contagion to this world, one might well ask, what is this quintessence of dust?' I was held for many days, 'a little month', drifting aimless, time-streaming. Refrigerated. Dark and cold. In my cell, then. But now, looking back, it seems only an 'hour of quiet' ruptured by interruptions. My vitality wasting, I floated past nihilism. Right now, I'm photocopying, but in the dream, I spoke out loud to no one in particular, I offered an apostrophe on 'how weary, stale, flat and unprofitable seem to me all the uses of this world' and how odd 'that it should come to this'. At other times, 'bounded in a nutshell', I danced alone.

Each day seemed the same, and they tortured me and interrogated me, and I lost track of time. But, instead of recording my dream, I began photocopying home appliance manuals, because soon I had to leave. And one day, after torture, they said, 'Unless you tell us what we want to know, we will shoot you. This is your final warning.' And that day, like every day, I repeated myself, and said that I didn't know what to tell them, that I had nothing to hide, nothing to say, that I didn't know what to say. I offered only my 'wild and whirling words'. Later, while I was photocopying, I thought perhaps, they *could* have listened to something about my destitute situation, perhaps something about how I had received a summons and was copying manuals for home appliances, but then I thought, *no*, I could not have *known* about the photocopying in the *dream*, because I had the dream the night *before*, and here I am photocopying *now*, and it is the night *after* the dream, and in any case, I am sure they would have been uninterested in the details of my home appliance manuals. In my dream, I danced through 'infinite space'. And in my dream, I danced alone. And then, without warning, they burst into my cold cell, and dragged me from darkness into liquid sunlight, a sunlight that seeped into my eyes. They half-walked me and half-dragged me into the courtyard, my eyes stung by seeping brightness, dragged me across pebble-strewn ground, vision dazzled, washed by light, I could only look down at the pebble-covered ground, and the pebbles all seemed exactly the same, perfect copies of each other, and the uniformed men with rifles erect standing before me were perfect copies of each other, and the wall stood pock-marked and red stained behind me. I knew they had placed me on the exact spot they had placed so many others before me, and they paused and asked me again if I had anything to say, and it felt like a dream to me, though 'a dream itself is but a shadow', and a wave of cold rushed over my body. All I could muster was an apostrophe, and all I could say was, 'So, this is how it feels to be in front of a firing squad.' And I was surprised and disappointed at the vacancy of my own self-centredness, and I chastised myself for my failure in casting some barbed quip, or rhetorical repartee, a *beau geste*, some jester's wit, perhaps a comment on the clouds overhead, for by now my swimming eyes had adjusted to the light and I looked to the heavens. I could have declared that one cloud swimming past took the 'shape of a camel', or no, perhaps 'more a weasel', or more precisely, 'very like a whale'. I could have announced something, anything. A pronunciamento. I could have spilled out that Hamlet's problem is not so much that he is mad or that he thinks too much, or that he hesitates, rather, it is that he thinks only too well, too clearly, and he thinks things through in full detail until he realizes with great sadness that there is no exit, and yet he is vivacious, vital, vehement, a passionate nihilist. And I could've said, 'O, woe is me, to have seen what I have seen, see what I see!' And, it could be said that we would all die of the truth, if the truth were truly known, and if it were not for literature. And perhaps this was Freud's great discovery, but it seems to me that it makes more sense to do a Shakespearean reading of Freud, than a Freudian reading of Shakespeare, and it seems that perhaps Jones, or Bloom, or Kristeva may have already thought of this, and all I'm doing is repeating, but it bears scrutiny, it bears thought, and as I'm photocopying, I remember that I stood dumbfounded, chastising myself for being unable to say anything beyond 'So, this is how it feels to be in front of a firing squad.' I could hear waves lapping at a nearby shore, and somehow, I knew that it was noon. And I heard the barking command, and heard the pounding shots, and I watched the crooked smile of the commander through puffs of smoke pouring from identical rifle barrels, speaking leaden words to my rising heart, and then, they came to untie me, while I stood awash, dumb, beneath a silence in the heavens. And they untied me and dragged me back out of the compound. Their sense of torture had induced them to use blanks in their rifles, and they threw me back into my cold cell, where each day seems like every other day, and here I am now, still photocopying instead of inking my way through a novel about, say, war, or sex, or death.

And although I'm photocopying manuals for home appliances, I could be writing about what happened last night when I was at the bar with my friends, Fortner and Larry and Horatio, and so, I'm copying, and I would've loved to have told *them* about my dream about the firing squad, but I hadn't *had* the dream yet. I did not have that dream until *after* I saw my friends last night at the bar. And, instead of writing in my diary and recording the story of what happened with Fortner, and Larry, and Horatio, I am photocopying home appliance manuals. And in the dream, one day had become very much like the next, until one day, they threatened me. 'Unless you tell us what we want to know, we will shoot you, and *this* time we're not joking. This time we will *really* shoot you. The last time was just a *warning*. This is your final chance.' And even though this was a repetition, the threat seemed very real, but, I still didn't know what to tell them, and I thought perhaps they could have listened to my story about how I received a summons, and had to leave my home, but of course, those thoughts came to me while I was photocopying, long *after* the dream, and much too late. And again, without warning, they smashed open the steel door to my cell, and half-walked and half-dragged me into the courtyard where the liquid sun dazzled my eyes, dragged me over ground strewn with pebbles, with bright light stinging my eyes, and each pebble on the ground looked the same, and a row of identical men in uniform stood erect before me with rifles in hand, and again, the wall stood behind me, the same wall with the same pock-marks and blood-soaked splatter stains. And again they asked if I had anything to say, and again all I could think of was how it felt like a dream. And as I'm photocopying manuals, I remember feeling a wave of cold, and all I could say to myself, more than to anyone else was, 'So, this is how it feels to be in front of a firing squad.' And again, I was surprised and disappointed in the vacancy of my own mental reaction, and though I was resolved to die, I chastised myself for not pronouncing some droll waggery, some erudite peroration, a witty sobriquet followed by an epistemological riff on the epiphenomenon of being. I could have said, 'A man may fish with the worm that hath eat of a king and eat of the fish that hath fed of that worm.' But, I did not. *Anything* would've been better than nothing, because it was certain that *this* time they would kill me. And, I am photocopying, and I *could* have said something like, 'In both writing and death, we are the victims of our own anonymous passivity ...' or, 'We would all die of the truth, if the truth were truly known, and if it were not for literature, and so, we are left with those soothsayers, Hypatia, Cervantes, Dante, Shakespeare and the other commentators ... Kant, who understands the importance of immanence ...' And I'm copying, and thinking of the sublime *noumena* of being, the immanence of Falstaff, with his crooked but jovial exterior, and his murderous licentious bloody self, and I'm thinking of how we are left with the ambivalence of Hamlet and the question of whether the ghost of his father was less a warning and more a trap, and I wonder about the fruitless and misguided warnings that Ophelia received from her brother and her father. And I consider others who, like Hamlet, are richly undecided about life, and it seems that perhaps Irigaray, or Cixous, or Baudrillard already said this, and I *could* have said that 'Writing negates the naïve existence of what it names and must therefore do the same to itself, simultaneously trivial and apocalyptic ...' And while I'm photocopying, I think of Heraclitus's river, and Beatrice 'Bice' di Folco Portinari who inspired

Dante Alighieri, and John Cage's *Silence*, and Blanchot's *Death Sentence* and *Thomas the Obscure* and how he once said that it seems both comical and miserable that a manifestation of a dread so potent that it splits open the heavens to storm upon us still requires the humble scribe at table inking letters on the page. But words escape me, and I remain enslaved by a dreadful silence, and the nearby waves lap against the shore, and somehow, I know that it is noon. And I'm photocopying, repeating some simulacrum, but it bears scrutiny, it bears thought. And I find myself gazing at the commander's crooked smile, and again I watch small puffs of smoke pour from identical rifle barrels speaking to my heart, and the world is emptied of everything. The sun wheel stops in mid-heaven, and a motionless being stands at my side, a silent immobility envelops me, the liquid calm of the universe condenses, the effervescent chaos of the noonday sun resounds, mingles with silence, is compressed by an all-encompassing peace. I remain without movement or thought, locked in a timeless purgatory, watching my execution, eyes half-closed, cheeks flushed, mouth half-open pouring out a final breath under the solar glare. The opaque corpse next to me increases in density, immanent in silence. The noon hour undermines any thought of flight. Time itself is deranged.

And again, they were using blanks, and as I knelt there gasping for breath, they seized my arms and shoulders and half-dragged half-walked me back to my cold cell where each day seems like another, and instead of recording my dream, or inking a novel about war, or sex, or death, I am photocopying manuals for home appliances and drinking ice-cold vodka because I must vacate, because I'm broke and have received a summons, and must move out, and it occurred to me that a summons is a sort of warning, and that there is something civilized about all of that. And last night at the bar with Fortner and Larry, and

Horatio and Ophelia, and no, the resonance of that name does not escape me, Ophelia was there too, not the Ophelia of *Hamlet*, not the Ophelia who lay in water singing, 'incapable of her own distress'. No, not the mermaid-Ophelia borne upon the waters, 'her clothes spread wide', carrying her over the waves. Not even the Ophelia drawn down to muddy death by 'garments, heavy with their drink'. No. Rather, Ophelia of the bar, another Ophelia, who said something that repeats in my mind, about how her father was a resistance fighter in the Ukraine, and how they were trapped between the Russians and the Germans, and how they got a choice between being conscripted or being executed. And I'm photocopying. And they were given fair warning and a choice between being shot or thrown into a mass mud grave, and so, her father accepted a job with the local military police, her father, against his will, took the job, but worked as a double agent. And I'm photocopying page after page remembering Ophelia's words, but not recording them, because I have not received permission to voice her words, and I don't know the name of the father, nor would I recognize it if I heard it, and her father passed warnings to as many as he could, when there was time, warnings that they were to be arrested, tortured, interrogated, shot, or sent to the icefields of Siberia. And I'm copying, and though he worked for the occupying forces, he sent signs, signs of warning, but the signs were never the same. And I'm copying. And the signs could never be the same because then the local authorities might get wise to him, and he could never say in advance what the sign would be, but it would be definite and clear. And I'm copying, and the villagers had to be ready to leave at a moment's notice, 24 hours a day from that moment onward, and they all lived in fear. And I'm copying page after page, and when the war was over, he landed on Pier 21, not Pier 22, Pier 21 in Canada, and there was a huge crowd of Polish and Ukrainian refugees on the dock, and somebody called his name, but it was his nickname, the same name he used in the police, his Chekist name, and I'm photocopying these manuals, and this person rushed to Ophelia's father, on Pier 21, after leaving war-torn Europe behind, and at first, Ophelia's father was frightened, but then this man dropped to his knees and began crying, 'How can I thank you?' And I'm copying, and it was one of the fellows he'd promised to warn, one who escaped with his family, but the strange thing was Ophelia's father had never warned *this* fellow, had not heard about the hit on *this* man, perhaps because after some time the authorities suspected Ophelia's father of being a double agent, so they never told him, and it turned out that on that very night the wind flipped open and shut the man's shutters twice, very loudly, very clearly, and very definitely, and I'm copying all of this. And then the shutters rested in silence, as before. And it was only the wind, slamming the man's shutters twice, and no more, but the man took it as a sign, *the* signifier. *He* knew a 'hawk from a handsaw', and he packed up his family and they disappeared into the night and headed through the forest, and stumbled across bogs, and along black back roads, eventually to a train station, finally to the coast, and out of the country, across the ocean to Canada, and here he was on Pier 21, and Ophelia's father stood dumbfounded before him. There never *was* a warning, there was no signifier, no signified, only the father's silent belief, and I'm copying. Somehow the wind had jumped the gun, and here they were, without Ophelia's father knowing about it, and the authorities who were looking for double agents afterward deduced that Ophelia's father could not have passed on the warning, because he didn't know about the planned arrest. They had deliberately kept him in the dark. But they did not know it was only the wind, the wind 'north by northwest', slamming the shutters, and so instead, without warning, they burst through some doors in the middle of the night, arrested, interrogated, tortured, and shot two *other* men who *did* know about the hit, shot two other men they suspected as double agents, and right now, a northerly wind is blowing rain outside, and I am photocopying.

And I am beginning to *read* the manuals even as I copy them, and the manuals are providing an explanation about the sounds you may hear from your home appliances, and I'm copying, and I'm drinking cold vodka reading the instruction manual as fast as I can while I slowly flip through the pages as I photocopy. I'm looking for some sign, and the words on the page are speaking to me, and the refrigerator manual has a section titled 'Understanding the Sounds You May Hear' which describes the various noises that might emerge from your home appliance, and even ventures to suggest what you might think of such sounds, and what they might mean, and the beautiful thing of it is, as I am photocopying, the sounds are discussed, defined and explained in *three* different languages: French, English, and Spanish. Upon reading these, I wish I could have repeated the sounds the night before when speaking to Fortner, and Larry, Horatio, and Ophelia, or I could have uttered those sounds when faced by the firing squad. I note that while the English version has a common-sense practicality to it, the French and especially the Spanish versions are far more mellifluous and onomatopoeic. And although I do not speak Spanish, I can repeat the sounds and understand enough to be enchanted by the semantic rhythms which carry a Cagean cacophony, or maybe a Dali-esque Surrealist flamenco flavour that effervesces under the flashing light of the photocopier and comes alive in my mind's ear in the form of an impromptu concert for philharmonic orchestra, jazz ensemble and eighty-eight refrigerators, and I'm copying, but don't ask why it is *eighty-eight* refrigerators, except that the number seems preposterously impossible, and there would be one refrigerator for each key on the piano keyboard, and eighty-eight is a repeating number, and it is the number of the house I must vacate, but other than that it has no special significance, except perhaps it is a symbol of death and rebirth, or infinity, and silence and infinity. And while I am photocopying the manual for the fridge, I realize that the section titled 'Understanding the Sounds You May Hear' is a gentle form of warning, a codification of a mechanical language, a language few may grasp or understand. And, here, as a courtesy, is detailed explication of sounds that might otherwise elude one's ken, sounds that under certain circumstances—say, in the pitch dark of night— might be misinterpreted, or cause concern, or fear, or panic, if these sounds were not translated. 'Forewarned, is forearmed,' thought I. And suddenly, I realized that this was an epistemologically laden document, rich in immanence on the *noumena* of being, fecund with meanings extending far beyond the limits of household refrigeration, for, after all, how could anyone explain all of the ambiguous sounds emanating from a refrigerator in the middle of the night, and name and number and identify and catalogue them all in a manual? What kind of person attends to the functioning cycles of a refrigerator for what must be at least a period of a month, listening and carefully deciphering and finally documenting all possible noises that emanate from the appliance, and then sits down to record those sounds in three different languages? And, yet *here*, under the flashing repeating light of the photocopier are references to the 'buzz-buzz' whirrings of spyro-gyro-valves, concatenations of thermostatically controlled refrigerator acoustics, fluctuations of chlorofluorocarbon refrigerant through pipelines, pulsating sounds of high-pitched, high-efficiency compressors, sizzling sounds, with hisses caused by defrost heaters, fan motors turning on, or shutting off, 'hunka-hunka' circulations, while the refrigerator and freezer compartments cycle air or liquid, accompanied by comments on *environmental* issues—not simple matters of chlorofluorocarbons rising like unspoken words into the invisible silence of the night air, but physical *environmental* issues, including the *acoustics* that result from hard surfaces such as wooden floors as opposed to linoleum, hardwood versus drywall, tile as opposed to laminate, which can reflect or deflect sounds with almost drum-like consistencies, so that 'the sounds seem louder than they actually are'—and I think, 'Though this be madness, yet there is method in it,' and I was amazed by this discovery that sounds can 'seem louder than they actually are'. I drank another small glass of icy vodka to celebrate this wonderful news, but more beautiful than this common-sense and practical information is the fact that water, when channelled through pipes during a defrosting cycle, might produce a sound that in the French version is defined as a *grésillement ('l'eau qui goutte sur les serpentins de condensation peut provoquer un grésillement')*, yes, a *'grésillement'* and silly without sleep, my mind still adumbrated with dreams of firing squads and war refugees warned by clapping window shutters, I begin to read the French and Spanish versions out loud. I begin to recite, *'Las vibraciones son causadas por el refrigerante que fluye en la tubería de agua'* and, *'Chaque fois que le programme se termine, vous pouvez entendre un gargouillement dans votre réfrigérateur.'* Yes! A *'gargouillement!'* And, of course, it was a perfect sign, a representation, a duplication, a semiotic rendition, and I knew, suddenly I realized that all this time, the refrigerator had been *talking* to me, and the refrigerator was my *mother*, and if I was put before the firing squad one more time, I would scream, 'The funeral baked meats, did *coldly* furnish forth the marriage tables,' or if someone was at my feet thanking me for saving their life from the cold icefields of Siberia, 'in the dead vast and middle of the night', with only the wind clapping their shutters, then I would remark, take heart: 'There's a special providence in the fall of a sparrow. If it be now, 'tis not to come; if it be not to come, it will be now; if it be not now, yet it will come: the readiness is all.' But instead, I am standing here ready and waiting, photocopying, and, before the firing squad shoots, I understand that the sounds of their rifles might seem louder than they actually are, and I will explain to them, that we would all die of the truth, if the truth were known, and I will tell them why it makes sense to do *not* a *Freudian* reading, but instead a *Shakespearean* reading of appliance manuals, for only in this way can we address the irresolvable gap between the self and Other, the unfathomable lack beyond the name-of-the-father, the *manqué a être* at the core of being, and how the *gargouillement* is part of a metonymic chain of desire, that can never be reached because desire, by definition, is that which is perpetually out of reach, for the sublime immanence of *noumena* and the flux and the acoustics arising from *las vibraciones por el refrigerante* can reveal the vital nihilism of *la tubería de agua*, and the ontic and the ontological are merely elements in a grand unification theory of the inevitable unpredictability of the *grésillement* of unrequited passion, and ultimately, even if things seem disparate or divided, like identical pebbles in a firing-squad courtyard, the simulacra can be recognized as being joined through their antagonism, initially under the guise of a crooked smile and a jovial exterior, but with a murderous and licentious and blood-sodden inner self. But I am not before a firing squad, and I'm not writing a novel about war, or death, or sex, and I'm not recording my dream, or the story that Ophelia recounted.

Instead, I am photocopying a refrigerator manual, and a summons has been sent, and I no longer have permission to remain, and if one does a Shakespearean reading, not a Freudian reading, then it is clear that I shall have to leave behind the refrigerator, as we must all leave our mothers, but what of Ophelia? And I remain hungry for meaning, but have eaten too much to care, yet there remains a rage for order that can only be defined through a full concert with philharmonic orchestra, jazz ensemble and the *gargouillement* of eighty-eight running refrigerators. Or, perhaps instead, a cold Cagean minimalist serendipity, as when the rain-drenched wind clearly and definitively slams two shutters twice and no more, and a family is spared, but without warning, two innocent men are executed, and 'Rosencrantz and Guildenstern are dead', but what seems separate or discrete is really interconnected, an extension, a simulacrum, a copy, a repetition of some *thing*, somewhere else, awaiting interpretation, and, 'the rest is silence ...'

———

Misappropriations

'How weary, stale, flat, and unprofitable/Seem to me all the uses of this world!' *Hamlet*, 1, 2.

'That it should come to this!' *Hamlet*, 1.2.

'A little month, or ere those shoes were old,/With which she follow'd my poor father's body'. *Hamlet*, 1, 2.

'These are but wild and whirling words, my lord.' *Hamlet*, 1, 5.

'Buzz buzz!' *Hamlet*, 2, 2.

'Though this be madness, yet there is method in't.' *Hamlet*, 2, 2.

'I am but mad north-north-west: when the wind is southerly, I know a hawk from a handsaw.' *Hamlet*, 2, 2.

'Do you see yonder cloud that's almost in shape of a camel?' *Hamlet*, 3, 2.

''Tis now the very witching time of night,/When churchyards yawn and hell itself breathes out/Contagion to this world: now could I drink hot blood.' *Hamlet*, 3, 2.

'How weary, stale, flat, and unprofitable/Seem to me all the uses of this world!' *Hamlet*, 1, 2.

'Thrift, thrift, Horatio! The funeral baked meats/Did coldly furnish forth the marriage tables.' *Hamlet*, 1, 2.

'In the dead vast and middle of the night.' *Hamlet*, 1, 2.

'And yet, to me,/what is this quintessence of dust?' *Hamlet*, 2, 2.

'A dream itself is but a shadow.' *Hamlet*, 2, 2.

'O, woe is me, To have seen what I have seen, see what I see!' *Hamlet*, 3, 1.

'A man may fish with the worm that hath eat of a king, and eat of the fish that hath fed of that worm.' *Hamlet*, 4, 3.

'This grave shall have a living monument:/An hour of quiet shortly shall we see.' *Hamlet*, 5, 1.

'There's a special/providence in the fall of a sparrow. If it be now,/'tis not to come; if it be not to come, it will be/now; if it be not now, yet it will come: the/readiness is all.' *Hamlet*, 5, 2.

'Rosencrantz and Guildenstern are dead.' *Hamlet*, 5, 2.

'The rest is silence.' *Hamlet*, 5, 2.

HUNGRY GHOSTS

Words stagger under the weight of time, under inadequate metaphors of space. Our language asks us to look forward to the future. But for the Andean Aymara people living on the altiplano, it is reversed. The future is behind us and has always been so. Imagine you are in a boat, looking forward, drifting downstream. What is to be comes towards you. Turn about and sit facing upstream. A simple pivot. The future is now behind you. It was always there. Does direction matter? Perhaps. Some of us carry the past as if it is something behind us. Wait a moment, look, listen. You'll see and hear how the past is always *before* you.

It is as if another hand is writing these words. As if another hand is moving the pen over my page almost too quickly for me to keep up.

It begins at my old family home. That home was similar to the house in which I live today. My current house sits nestled on a quiet thoroughfare in a quiet town, not too far from the Golden Horseshoe, several hours' drive from my first home in Toronto's west end near Jane and Bloor streets. That first home had a white stucco exterior, and it was surrounded by oak trees, with the nearby Humber River leading to Lake Ontario. I remember painting the stucco each year to keep it fresh.

The little white house where I live now is different. It used to be a humble church, but it was decommissioned before I moved in. Maybe 'chapel' is a better word, because the building is small. It's considerably smaller than my former house in Toronto. This house is a rectangular bungalow with a steep roofline, steeper than expected for a small city bungalow. But the steep roof provides ample attic space, well-suited for storage. The main floor boasts an open-concept arrangement with conjoined living room and kitchenette, and there's a bathroom and bedroom partition on the side. The basement is open and runs the full length of the bungalow. At one time, a ten-foot-tall wooden steeple was perched at the front of the roof. A driveway leads to a parking area at the back of the property, and there's more parking on the street.

If you park on the street, then you might get a ticket, but police generally overlook cars parked in front of a church on Sundays. By the time I bought this building, the previous owner had removed the steeple. He didn't want to attract parishioners. I drove by this little house regularly, and I remember the steeple.

Even after they decommissioned the chapel, strange things continued to happen. The former owner claimed he heard knocks at the front door, but on answering the sounds, was met only by a cool breeze. In bed, half asleep, he heard footsteps in the converted living room, creaking floorboards, and sometimes a muffled choir. Other times he swore he heard people crying, or footsteps in the attic. After several weeks of such occurrences he became confused, couldn't tell dream from actuality. He decided to sell.

I bought this house according to my mother's fortune-telling. This house was in the cards. I imagined the building when it was still a chapel, pictured its floor plan. It was simple. A rectangle with rows of pews. I imagined an altar near the back, not quite against the back wall, but far enough from it to muffle noises that might come from outside. It got me thinking. When they pass on, some people don't realize it. They return to familiar haunts. Past. Future. Looking back. Looking forward.

I remember our old house. My father worked in construction and was rarely home. I went to school and did odd jobs. My mother was a bookkeeper at the Wedgewood Restaurant at Jane and Bloor, but she moonlighted as a caterer. She studied cookbooks, recipes, memorized the best and improvised the rest. She did everything by hand, dipping fingers into sauces, intuitively adding spices. I watched her work while I peeled hard-boiled eggs, potatoes, or sometimes shrimp. But it was the *way* she presented her buffets that drew customers.

She turned cooking into an art. No detail was too small. She crafted little penguins out of boiled eggs, with black olive heads, oval wings sliced from olive edges, triangular beaks fashioned from bits of carrot. She crafted flowers from diced radishes left overnight in spring water. Carrot trees with expanding branches were topped with bunches of curly parsley. Edible gardens. Miniature savannahs. Pickle-crocodiles patrolled the salads, their cranberry eyes lurking amidst sour cream and herring salads. Floral patterns emerged from paper-thin turnip slices she'd trimmed with pinking shears, hued with food colouring. Shavings of English cucumber imitated leaf patterns amidst faux roses, poppies, anemones and floral garnishes in a magical culinary landscape, a *terra incognita* waiting for discovery. She worked in a time before veganism. I sympathize; my son and many friends are now vegan, and I have moved to a vegetarian diet as I slip towards vegan myself. But I don't apologize for her creations which arose from a different ethos. The delightful scents seduced you. I often stood hovering over her foodscapes: maple-syrup-glazed baked salmon stuffed with crabmeat, adorned with wafer-thin citrus curls; lobster thermidor with egg yolk, brandy, Gruyère and hollandaise; fresh pike with minced mushroom and egg, combined with chopped onion, nutmeg, cardamom, and horseradish on the side; Arctic char with smoked almond Romesco sauce, thinly sliced pan-seared almonds; fillets of trout with Bercy sauce splashed with a white-wine reduction, chopped shallots, simmered in a velouté and thickened with blonde roux; arrays of smoked eel slipping through lemongrass. The latter was *de rigueur* among the Balts. Many consider eels horrific, but they are celebrated by gourmets. And always, as a gesture to the olden times, gefilte fish, sweetened using beets, the old-fashioned way.

She learned how to prepare gefilte fish and other recipes in Daugavpils. Gefilte fish was popular among her Ashkenazi neighbours and friends. Daugavpils, sometimes called Niyar-Palin, or Dvinsk, one-time home of the painter Rothko, hovered near the Lithuanian border. My mother worked at a tannery there before the war.

Before she escaped, her brothers were sent to Siberia. Exiled. They went from all to nothing, their bodies wasting on the infamous 'exquisite' diet, composed of a few calories less than required daily for a human body to remain alive. My uncles, crushed by the weight of hunger, awaited release. How my mother would've cooked for them! They all died. They grew ill before starving to death. Freezing temperatures. Forced labour. Subsistence food. Organ collapse. Lung or heart complications. Liver or kidney failure. Those sorts of deaths suited the warden's goal. When reps from the Red Cross toured the camps, the coroner's reports indicated organ failure, not starvation. This allowed them to avoid any unpleasantness involving the Geneva Convention. My uncle Peter sent letters from Taiseta, in the Irkutsk region of the Gulag. He was sent to the ice region. Others were sent to labour and die in salt mines. My uncle and those others shared a common fate. I saved my uncle's letters—fragile paper triangles without envelopes. He begged for food. We thought of sending garlic cloves, macaroni, rice, nuts, chocolate, beans, oatmeal, *anything* that might survive the postal journey to the icy barb-wired camp. We sent food packages, but surely they were taken by the guards. There are stories of mass graves. Three to a grave, with only one marker. It kept the numbers down. Others were lost entirely. I've watched videos of lines of prisoners kneeling along edges of long ditches, hands tied behind their backs. Riflemen systematically walking up to shoot them through the base of the skull. One after another. The impact of the bullets buffeting them into the ditch. Others died less pleasantly. Starvation, organ failure, ice. Lost lives. Lost futures. It's their hands that move my pen today. Ghost hands, hungry to tell their story. A future-passed.

The Aymara people recognize the difference between what is known and not known. They think of it as a key to perception. What is known lies before you, can be experienced through eyes, ears, nose, hand. What is known is the past. The past lies before you. But the unknown, the future, lies behind you, where it can't be seen or heard. So say the Aymara.

Some days, I feel hungry ghosts behind my back. Today, I'm on the front porch of my little white house, sitting on my old three-legged wooden stool. I call this stool my 'cricket' because it squeaks when I sit on it. The street is quiet today, but I know that the ghosts are not far behind. Sometimes, they pop up in front of you. The quicker you run, the faster they chase you. The past returns to face you. But that is another story. This one is more cheerful.

After the war, my mother became obsessed with food. She dove into the world of cuisine. I set the tables at her buffets. Her presentations were works of art. Her salads were as diverse as they were imaginative: roasted cauliflower with a white béchamel sauce; coleslaw with red apples and caraway seeds; beet salad with sour cream, green onion and spiced mayonnaise; red cabbage with chopped onions, vegetable oil and dry red wine; potato salad with diced boiled eggs and creamy Dijon dressing, diced celery and parsley; herring salad or *rossol* with pickled beets, diced fresh apples, lemon juice and yogurt; salt herring with chopped dill pickles, topped with sour cream and chives; Waldorf salad with fresh apples, celery, seedless grapes and walnuts, all dressed to go in a lemon mayonnaise sauce perched atop a bed of red butterhead lettuce. Nearby lay expanses of thinly sliced beef and ham rolled into tubes, stuffed with cream cheese and chives, garnished, and set atop silver salvers in geometric patterns. All this interspersed with platters of freshly cut vegetables arranged in spirals, concentric circles, or S-shaped swirls. Subtly delicious aromas arose as I approached such delicacies: turkey roulades stuffed with fennel, thyme, tarragon, puréed meats, shallots and chopped egg; braised chicken with sherry vinegar, prunes and cream; roast duck with garlic and wild mushrooms. The ends of the buffet tables were splashed with rainbows of inviting fresh berries nestled inside hollowed cantaloupe halves cut with zig-zag edges. There were mock strawberry trees, pineapples carved with monkey faces, multi-coloured assortments of melon balls dancing atop verdant layers of crisp lettuce. And, my favourite, the pastries: cream puffs, éclairs, cakes, tortes, chocolate bombs, and always, my mother's homemade Black Forest cake topped with small peaks of hand-whipped, sweetened heavy cream, Kirsch-soaked cherries and chocolate shavings. Ingredients for her batter included buttermilk, espresso and walnuts. For her, such labour was an epicurean expedition.

She became known in the ethnic community, was in high

demand among Balts. They nicknamed her 'salt of the earth' for her hard work, imaginative displays and surprising savours. Her buffets were served at room temperature, no need to pre-heat. We would load my father's '56 Ford Fairlane with stackable wooden box trays that he built at a carpenter friend's workshop. I tagged along to the carpenter's shop, bored, and watched as the bandsaw cut sheets of plywood to be assembled into stackable boxes, each one just deep enough to hold four large oval platters. My mother used upright toothpicks to protect her decorations and glazes from clear plastic wrap. My mother's catering was in demand for anniversaries, milestone birthdays, weddings and, of course, funerals. She'd adjust the tone of her creations to match the occasion. Brighter tones for happier times, more muted but still imaginative hues to honour those who had passed. Her meals would be served in the homes of wealthier clients, or in rented guest halls, or sometimes in church basements, for those who were not quite as well off. I helped carry the trays, unload the platters and set the tables. We always said a prayer after the tables were set.

She started at three in the morning, preparing buffets due by five or six in the evening. She always had a helper or two. Often, our nanny lent a hand with those tasks and made a bit of extra pocket money for helping in the kitchen. We called her Omi. My mother frequently worked late at the restaurant, so after school she engaged Omi to care for my sister and me. In her youth, Omi had been a successful actress. She performed on stage in Riga, was quite a man-eater in her day, and she loved to play pranks. How she laughed, and fed us, and chased us, me and my sister, all around the entire house. I sometimes took cover beneath the dining room table, exhausted, while she threatened to kiss me. At her 80th birthday, she spoke to a gathering of friends, and said proudly that she'd chase and kiss me again, except her arthritis was acting up and her new shoes were pinching. Otherwise, I'd be in a lot of trouble. Sometimes she'd watch soap operas on our old RCA Victor TV. After twenty years in Canada, she still spoke broken English and preferred 'the old language'. I asked her why she watched TV when she barely understood the words. She said that she'd worked onstage for years, and now she just made up her own plotlines and dialogues.

She was a natural comedienne. One time at dinner, my mother decided to serve Reddi-wip in an aerosol can. Normally, my mother would never consider serving anything other than hand-whipped cream. It would begin with my mother dispatching me to the store with orders to bring back a container with the correct fat percentage. I never understood the differences or the concentrations. Even after I'd been told which container to buy, I'd stand in the aisle blankly staring at the percentages marked on different cream cartons. 10%, 25%, 30%, 36%. Inevitably, I'd fumble the task and bring home the wrong percentage, only to be scolded and immediately sent back to apologetically ask for an exchange. When feeding our family, my mother wouldn't think of serving store-bought whipped cream, but often, she was overburdened. So, one time she made an exception. There never seemed to be enough hours in her days to get things done. Preparing Sunday meals was an uphill struggle. One Sunday, as we finished supper, she served us strawberry shortcake for dessert, and, hiding her embarrassment, brought out a can of Reddi-wip. The label on the can proudly proclaimed, 'Made with Real Cream'. My sister and I grabbed the can and sprayed our cakes. To us, the difference between store-bought and hand-wrought was minimal. Some people may not know it, but the aerosol propellant in those cans is nitrous oxide, 'laughing gas', the same as used by dentists. Omi started giggling watching us spray dollops of white cream onto our desserts. I passed the can, but the vaudevillian in Omi couldn't help it. She shot a spray in my face. I laughed, tried to grab the can but she was surprisingly nimble, and let loose a shot at my sister. My mother spewed a horrified laugh. My father stared in disbelief. Omi, laughing out of control, passed the can back to me. I paused, used my shoulder to wipe a wad of cream from my face, and fired. The shot hit her neck. Omi grabbed the can back, arose ceremoniously, and circled the table anointing each of us. Before dessert was done, mounds of whipped cream garnished our faces and the table. My mother never brought the stuff again. Not while Omi was there.

In those days people gossiped about how Omi walked everywhere. She couldn't drive and couldn't be bothered with the city's transit system. She was remarkably fit for someone in her eighties. She walked all the way from north of St. Clair to Bloor West to do her shopping. She didn't have to speak English much. She'd just walk in, pick out groceries and plunk money on the counter, money from her old folks' pension or from her daughter. The people behind the counter weren't much better with English. They were Eastern European or maybe Chinese or Korean, also escapees, also DPs. Displaced people. She wasn't shy, just illiterate, and then only in English. One time she sat down to tea with me and said things: 'I loved my home before the war. Here, I feel out of place, but my family is here, and I am here now.' She sighed. What could she do? So many of her old friends and family lay in mass graves. She, still a young woman then, knew it was time to leave when she witnessed bayonet disembowellings just up her street. More troops arriving. She hopped a train to a nearby town, but enemy troops were already there, so close. She joined a small group that escaped through the woods to a waiting cart and horse. Then travelled to the next town, and from there, onto a train. There was no time for goodbyes, no time for lost lives. Precious gifts were left behind. Grandfather's wooden chair, the tablecloth woven by her mother's hands, no time for memories. Death beckoned. Life awaited. Then, a boat to England. Then, across to Canada. What choice was there? She'd hear mutterings when shopping for groceries. 'Fucking immigrants.' Been here twenty years. She heard them. She tells me she can't be bothered learning English. Looks me in the eye, 'I understand enough, but I'm too old.' That automobile accident damaged her permanently. Some things you can't fix. Eventually, she died of complications. Shattered hip problems. At the funeral chapel, my sister and I stood by her casket. When no one was watching we hid a can of Reddi-wip under Omi's skirt near her left hand. Later, we joined the buffet downstairs.

On days when my mother was charging through yet another catering job, I'd watch from the kitchen door. She had worked with Omi as though they could read each other's minds. Their swift fingers turned the mundane into the wondrous. It was as if their hands had minds of their own. One morning, I recall it was a Friday, I was up early, and my mother gave me devilled eggs for breakfast. Devilled eggs were particularly popular at my mother's buffets, and she'd decorate each with a note of delight, sometimes a simple dash of paprika, other times, orange or black caviar, or an S-shaped slice of anchovy. And she served me a couple of bacon buns called *pirags*. For those who don't know, *pirags* are a special Latvian treat, a baker's delight. Start with lightly sautéed onions, pan-fried diced ham and bacon chunks, allow them to cool, then tuck them gently onto one side of a circular piece of bread dough. Fold over and top with a light egg-white glaze. Bake until light brown. The art of *pirags* is to make the bread thin while packing the insides with a wealth of tongue-delighting goodness.

It was the simple things we enjoyed most. My mother's kugel always seemed to be waiting for us. Sometimes she served it as a side dish, but it made a good snack by itself. It could be served cold, but warm from the oven was best, especially when topped with cold sour cream and chopped green onions. I sometimes helped in the kitchen, but my tasks were limited to peeling or stirring. One Friday morning, my mother asked me to peel a pot of boiled shrimp before I dashed off to class. I washed my hands and mumbled my usual litany of pointless protests as I perched atop the old three-legged stool in the dining room. Our dining room had aged wooden floors and sat next to the kitchen. On catering days, the dining room doubled as a workroom. By then, we had nicknamed the stool 'cricket'. I kept that three-legged stool after my mother died. Somehow, I found the squeak comforting. I dug into the large pot of jumbo shrimp, shelling them quickly. I had developed a moderate degree of expertise with these tasks. The water in the pot was still warm, but not hot. Through a mist of steam and inviting vapours, my mother shouted at me from the hectic kitchen, 'Be sure to put on an apron. You won't have time to change clothes before school.' I fired back a reply from the dining room, 'Yes, apron, okay, already wearing one.' I was lying of course. I saw no point in wasting time putting on an apron. I was quite familiar with peeling shrimp. No need for an apron. I proceeded with gusto, squeezing the tails, pulling and tossing the shells into a nearby cardboard box. I was used to this kind of work, and within a few minutes, I had shelled the mound of shrimp. In my dampened shirt, I charged off to school.

It was a grey autumn day and the schoolteacher's hand carefully shaped letters across the blackboard. Her flawless script provided directions for our next assignment. I sat at my usual desk in the middle aisle near the back of the classroom. I liked that spot. It wasn't quite at the back wall where the noisy delinquents gathered, but I was far enough away from the front to avoid frequent selection for answers to questions that I only half-understood. Arithmetic seemed simple enough, but the logic of algebra eluded me. And sometimes I could indulge my daydreams undetected, gazing through tree-branch shadows dancing on the nearby windowpane. Something was different that day. We copied the teacher's instructions into our blue-lined notebooks, but for some reason, those sitting in the aisles on either side of me started to turn in my direction. Even Peggy, the pigtailed girl who sat in front of me, turned about with a sour face. Peggy made a point of ignoring me whenever possible. It was like someone had dropped a pebble into a pond. Ever-expanding concentric circles of gazes turned my way. Back at the blackboard, the teacher paused in mid-notation. Her hand stopped as if it had a mind of its own, and for a moment she stood staring at the chalk in her fingers. Then, she turned to face us. 'Does anyone smell fish?' The class erupted.

Afterwards, during recess, my pal Frank offered to lend me some of his underarm deodorant spray. Frank worked as a bicycle delivery boy for Lingeman's, the local pharmacy. His task was sobering, requiring him to dutifully deliver prescription medications to those in need. Because he worked at Lingeman's, Frank was among the first in our group to discover health and grooming aids. I was grateful to him for his thoughtfulness, but instead ran home during lunch to change my clothes. At the time, my mother had popped out to the grocer's, but Omi was busy peeling potatoes. She teased me mercilessly and asked if I wanted to shell more shrimp before I returned to school. I don't think Omi ever told my mother about that fiasco, but if she did, they would've had a good laugh.

Not long ago, my mother passed away, returned to the

earth. She spent her final years in a retirement home. She often confided that, in her opinion, the food service at the retirement home was going downhill. I would visit and bring small pastries. She was a diviner and could see upstream and down. Sometimes after tea, she laid out my cards and told me what was behind me, what was before me. When she saw the ace of hearts, point up, she pronounced a change of life, a new house.

This new house was in the cards. It isn't quite like my old home in Toronto where my mother used to prepare buffets in our tiny kitchen. This house is set on a quiet thoroughfare several hours drive from my first home in Toronto's west end. Except, instead of a white stucco exterior, this house has white exterior panelling. And this house is not surrounded by tall oak trees, although there is a nearby river that flows into Lake Erie. And Lake Erie flows into Lake Ontario, which then flows into the Saint Lawrence River, which flows into the Atlantic.

One day, not long after I moved in, while poking around the attic, I found a good-sized wooden model of this house back from when it had been a chapel. The model was about three feet tall with a three-foot-square base. I decided to phone the former owner to ask him about it. Yes, he said, the model was resting in the attic when he moved in. He saw no harm in leaving it there. He explained that by the time he moved into the building, they had decommissioned the chapel, so it no longer served as a church. The congregation had increased in size, and they'd found another property. Upon decommissioning, the chapel was relegated to 'profane but not sordid use.' I wondered about the word 'profane', and when I looked it up, I discovered that it simply meant desacralized.

The former owner explained that, by the time he took possession of the building, the churchgoers had already removed the pews to serve in their new, larger church. He recounted how he had removed the wooden steeple at the front of the house. It was about ten feet tall, made of wood, but not particularly heavy because it was hollow inside. He had already spoken to me about the unexplained noises in the building before I bought the place, and he confided that he slept much better in his new house. All of this got me thinking about how many people might've been married, or baptized, or confirmed, or sent to their eternal rest when this building was still a chapel. I thought of people who might've died since then, and wondered if they might've returned, maybe to say goodbye, or just to revisit their old church before moving on. Moving on from all to nothing. Or maybe, from nothing to all. I thought of how some of them might suddenly find themselves in the afterlife, wanting to talk, or visit, or send a message. It's all right with me if they did. If they're friendly, it would be all right with me.

So, I thought about the little wooden model of what used to be a chapel and decided to move it from the attic. It was constructed to about one-tenth scale, an architect's model. When I handled it, I noticed that the roof was detachable, allowing me to examine the floor plan with its pews, nave and altar. The arrangement was much as I had imagined it. And, when I detached the main floor, I found the basement underneath. The basement was bare, with three little tables and a few miniature chairs set about the walls. There was a slightly raised floor at the far end of the basement which could serve as a small stage area. I'm sure that before it was purchased by the parishioners, this building must've been an ordinary bungalow with little to set it apart, other than a steeper-than-average roofline. Perhaps it was the roofline that attracted them. And so, they must've purchased it and converted it into a chapel only to decommission it years later. It's curious how such things have a way of coming and going.

To be fair to the man who used to live here, I *have* heard noises and experienced manifestations of what could be 'invisible visitors', including in the attic where I discovered the scale-model chapel. I thought that if a spirit returned at some point, then it might visit the little wooden model instead of the house itself. I might be able to mislead such spirit-guests and confine their visits to the model. So I put the model of the house-that-used-to-be-a-chapel on the front porch. I imagined that a visiting spirit might become frustrated or angry if it entered the building proper, since all vestiges of its function as a chapel had disappeared. But the scale model of the chapel was true to form, and spirits could find the original wooden pews, the altar and the nave, all in their proper places. And if such visitors descended to the little model's basement, then they would find a space closely resembling the original location set up for celebration or mourning. Such gatherings may once have been graced with buffets, much like the ones my mother used to prepare in other church basements.

And so, I re-situated the wooden model of the chapel on the front porch of this house. I was making it available for any passing spirits who might recognize it or drop by for a visit. I'm certain that for spirits, the size of a building doesn't matter much. Instead, it's the feeling, the vibration. And since the model was stored in the attic all this time, it must have absorbed the spirit of this place when it was still a chapel. I decided to conduct a little research on the subject.

I learned of an old Buddhist saying about hungry ghosts who can no longer fend for themselves, and I learned that it's to your mutual benefit to honour such spirits with gifts of food. The spiritual merit you gain feeding hungry shades is substantial, and the spirits are grateful and render kindnesses to the provider. Among Meso-Americans, neighbours to the Aymara,

Tlazolteotl, the Aztec goddess of earth, motherhood and fertility, redeems the soul of anyone confessing misdeeds by cleansing their spirit and devouring their sins. Traditions of sin-eating abound. In some communities, a corpse cake is placed atop the breast of the deceased, to be eaten by the nearest relative. In ancient times, when a sin-eater arrived, family members would come out with a low three-legged stool. The sin-eater would sit outside, facing the front door of the house. A family member would come out and give the sin-eater a silver coin, as well as a crust of bread to be eaten immediately, and then, a tankard of ale to be swallowed in a single draught. The sin-eater would then rise and declare the departed soul cleansed. For this, and for their service to others in the community, sin-eaters pawned their own souls. They were considered pariahs. I've heard stories about those who eat the sins of a sin-eater, but that is another tale.

I recall the ancient Lett belief that shades inhabit the place beyond the sun known as Aizsaule, overseen by maternal deities including the Earth-Mother and Wraith-Mother. Passageways leading to *that* beyond are found in forests, bogs, graveyards, caves, rivers, or lakes much like the little river near here that empties into Lake St. Clair. And in ancient times, every autumn, the souls of the departed were invited to a feast. Homes would be cleaned, and tables set. An elder invited the spirits, often calling them by name. The elder would usually begin by scolding the spirits for failing to adequately care for the house and its inhabitants, and then would ask them to try harder next year. Then, all who were present, including members of the family, were invited to eat. Following supper, the host asked the spirits to depart.

Based on what I discovered, I set tiny portions of food atop the little tables in the basement reception hall of the scale-model chapel. I included a small vial of spring water, a fragment of shortbread with ginger-nut biscuits, several sultana raisins, a single wedge of purple-stripe garlic, three pieces of orzo pasta, seven grains of basmati rice, three thimbles, one with Tuscan olive oil, another with oil of hyssop, and a third with wildflower honey. On one of the little tables, I placed a teaspoon of demerara sugar, a pinch of buckwheat flour, a dozen sunflower and pumpkin seeds, along with several hazelnuts and walnuts, a wedge of dark chocolate, five black-turtle beans, a tablespoonful of oatmeal, a capful of maple syrup, a pinch of manna and a dollop of mustard, on the side. I remember my parents used to send smaller assortments of dry goods to my uncle in the Gulag. We could tell by his despairing letters that those packets never reached him. But that was then. Meanwhile, atop the tiny table, I put some sprigs of sage from my garden, and next to them I placed some small pieces of paper with a couple of pencil stubs. And I left a dash of salt. Centuries ago, this entire region lay under an inland sea connected by a mighty river to the Atlantic. Now, this town is known for its production of automobiles and salt. There's an underground salt mine in the heart of town, producing mountains of rock salt for highway use in winter. Sometimes I throw a little salt over my left shoulder to ward off 'unwelcome visitors'. Salt of the earth. Look forward. Look back.

Sometimes at twilight, I sit atop the 'cricket' on my front porch. I sit beside the scale-model chapel awaiting the arrival of those who have already passed, and I look toward the future arrival of those who still are. Oh, and if you've recently departed, if you've left your home behind and you happen to come by my place, then you're welcome to visit the little chapel where the pews and nave await anyone who'd like to drop by, and rest, and maybe meditate. Afterwards, if you're hungry, you can slip downstairs to where a small buffet awaits.

LAYER CAKE:
MAYAKOVSKY'S BRAIN

A pistol shot. Perhaps another. A lover's quarrel. Suicide or murder? Shortly after, the forensic investigator is shot dead by an unknown assailant.

I was eating breakfast, thinking of historical events. Revolution. It doesn't matter where or when the revolution happens, but let's say, 20th-century Russia. I wonder if it matters how uncertainty arrives during political change, and whether people should feel free to openly express opinions at such times.

The characters involved unveil the ways in which the three-ring circus of politics, finance and sex warps our lives. The ending is always the same. Conflict, confusion, chaos and death. God-fearing, pro-governmental forces, tormented by rebels. Rebels resisting a corrupt ruling order that has fallen out of touch with the cast-iron, bull-crap realities of life. Revolution ignites in the marketplace. Amidst this explosion, two lovers. One, loyal to older values, but still espousing revolution. The second, passionate, half-mad, devoutly pro-revolutionary. They fall into each other's arms.

I became distracted while having breakfast. I watch television while eating alone. Today it was a replay of an older PBS documentary on the brains of great Russians, the Brain Institute in Moscow. Bolsheviks founded the Brain Institute in 1928 to gather a 'Pantheon of Brains', which might rival the Pantheon in Paris. The Institute dissected the brains of dozens of famous

Russians, including Eisenstein, Gorky, Mayakovsky, Lenin, Stalin and Sakharov. The Institute continued work until the collapse of the Soviet Union in 1989. Since then, holdings were only displayed for special visitors as a tribute to an earlier period.

It was the fourteenth day of April, in the year 1930, that Russian poet Vladimir Mayakovsky died. It is said that he died of a self-inflicted pistol shot in the bedroom of his Moscow flat. His closest friends, including the writer Yuri Olesha hurried to Mayakovsky's flat upon hearing the dreadful report. I've noticed that some scholars include Olesha with the Odessa School of Writers alongside others such as Isaac Babel. They all covered topic areas related to revolution and in many ways Mayakovksy's life. But, as the experts point out, writers' groups are often porous, their beliefs indeterminate. Olesha's novel *Envy* tells the story of Nikolai Kavalerov, a dismal young loser who rejects communist ideals, loathes the new laws of the land and is consumed by envy of his benefactor, Andrei Babichev, a model Soviet citizen who successfully supervises a sausage factory. Otto von Bismarck once said, 'Laws are like sausages, it is better not to see them being made.' But Olesha wasn't thinking of sausages the day that he sat in the parlour with others awaiting what they believed was the doctor's examination of Mayakovsky's body. Instead, Olesha was thinking of little things. Why salt can spill off a butter knife, leaving no trace, leave the blade shining, as if untouched. How the pince-nez that Isaac Babel sometimes wore looked like a bicycle. How, if you look carefully, all human beings are surrounded by tiny letters. Letters on the table before them, on their clothing, on their pince-nez if they have one, letters flying about their heads, nestling in their hair, resting on their shoulders like some scattered army of ants struggling to survive until they evolved, grew massive, became huge letters on the signs and billboards that surround us each day. Polonskaya and her husband sat there as well. Olesha was lost for words, so he remained silent, ruminating about letters. He knew that if he spoke, he would be unable to articulate his cascading ideas, and he would only blurt out unexpected words or leap-frogging thoughts. Instead, he imagined a red bouquet of floral letters exiting Mayakovsky's heart. But at that moment, Yuri Olesha's reverie on letters was disturbed by a loud cracking sound arising from Mayakovsky's bedroom.

In seconds, a doctor in a white lab coat rushed out of the bedroom carrying a small washbasin containing Mayakovsky's brain. As the doctor hurried by, ready to leap into a waiting automobile, he muttered something about the extreme size of the brain. The automobile whisked him and the organ away to the Moscow Brain Institute. Mayakovsky's body, *sans* grey-matter, was abandoned on the bloodstained carpet of the musty bedchamber. One of the group unkindly commented that the deceased had been a crackpot for years and now his brain was being carried away in a pot. After all, he was a Futurist upstart, a crazy-head poet-playwright agitator for social change who couldn't give a jack-ass fuck about the pretensions of bourgeois art, love or faith. His heart throbbed with a singular detestation for the doomed calamities of a hypocritical system.

But he loved. Was driven by an unrestrainable, rock-hard passion for Veronika Polonskaya, a rising star in the Moscow theatre. But Veronika was poised to marry another. And so, Vladimir fell into a frenzy. And while Veronika had enjoyed his passion, her fiancé, who eventually became her husband, declared that enough was enough. Revolution was fine, but the rebellion was over, and there wasn't much future in it. In addition, she craved the finer things, including a secure path to her own success. Unbridled passion was dandy, but there was more to life than political platitudes. Vlad was consistently unpredictable, volatile, uncontrollable, a great lover, but uneven, moody. So, Polonskaya married Mikhail Yanshin, a rising director. Vlad envisioned her as La Gioconda. He was poised to make an art theft. It had to be him, secret thief of Veronika's heart. He'd perform sexual larceny, steal her for himself. Veronika, flattered by Vlad's passion, let things drag. After she married Yanshin in 1926, she kept visiting Vlad, informing him that she had to break things off. He begged, threatened suicide. She revelled in his bohemian decadence, but Yanshin was stable, a growing success, had a future. She insisted that her relationship with Vladimir had to end. In desperation, Mayakovsky wrote 'Backbone Flute', a poem howling over a passionate love hurled at the feet of a woman who preferred the safe haven of domesticity and the social status provided by a dull, albeit successful, husband. The poem raged against fate's cruelty, promised death and suicide.

But Yanshin was not entirely dull. He'd played Lariosik in Bulgakov's *Days of the Turbins*. The play was directed by Stanislavski, and was based on Bulgakov's personal experience in Kiev in late 1919 and early 1920 at the height of the Russian Civil War, which dogged the heels of both Russian Revolutions in 1917. The first revolt erupted in the spring, with the overthrow of the imperial government. The second revolt broke out in autumn, placing the Bolsheviks in power. These uprisings, pursued by the Russian Civil War, left Red and White factions fighting for supremacy. The Old Guard struggled against the Bolsheviks. Communists battled capitalists. The Turbin family, swallowed by the turmoil, endured horrific personal tragedy as their world collapsed. Amidst indiscriminate violence, abandonment, anarchy, inconceivable betrayals, the Turbin family reunited to celebrate New Year's Day. The play was a roaring success. Audiences rose to standing ovations. Yanshin's star was on the rise.

Mayakovsky grew increasingly insane. A licentious lunatic-poet, beloved by the nation, unhinged and volatile, he raged fitfully. His erratic behaviour attracted Veronika, or at least the actress in her, but enough was enough. He was a careening meteor about to become a crater. Veronika wasn't going down with him. She'd consulted her Roma fortune teller.

It's here that my own family history is entwined. This was the same Roma woman who met my mother when she was but a girl and showed her the art of divination. It was this old Romany woman who advised Veronika that Mayakovsky's star was falling and Yanshin's was rising. Veronika preferred someone balanced, sane, reliable. After Mayakovsky's death, Yanshin proved the Roma diviner's prophecy by landing the position of Artistic Director at the Moscow Theatre of the Forest Industry. Soon after, he would direct the Romen Theatre, a key centre of Romany culture in Russia, and after that, he would be appointed as Chief Director of the Stanislavski and Nemirovich-Danchenko Moscow Academic Music Theatre, which featured ballets and operas including *Don Quixote*, *La Traviata* and *La Bohème*, along with more progressive productions such as Satie's *Socrate*. By 1934, Yanshin would divorce Veronika, but that didn't matter at the time.

Yanshin was present the day Mayakovsky died. It is said that Mayakovsky committed suicide. It is unknown how much Yanshin knew of the affair. Yanshin was a Red Guard volunteer in his youth. Bourgeois notions of marital fidelity were considered collateral damage following the Revolution. Some still believed in monogamy, if not for sanctity, then for convenience. It is here that versions of what happened diverge.

Some say things came to a head in the spring of 1930. Mayakovsky got a pistol to prove he meant suicidal business. At his flat, in a shouting match with Veronika, he madly waved the pistol, aimed it at his skull. His arm muscles twitched. His trigger finger pulsed. Veronika stood back in tears, watched, horrified, as he waved the gun at himself, then at her. She remained firm. He cursed outrageously, accusing her of deceitfully *acting* her love, charged her with *playing* her passion, called her a strumpet of the theatre, swore that *his* ardour was genuine, that it arose in the blood, in the fire burning his soul. He slammed his open palm onto the suicide note atop his writing desk. She broke out in tears but kept to the same tune. It had to end. For Vlad, it was the ultimate betrayal, an inconceivable slap in the face.

News of his death circulated quickly. Some reports announced that Veronika Polonskaya was leaving the flat when she heard a single shot behind Mayakovsky's closed door. She rushed back to find the poet collapsed on the floor surrounded by a growing pool of blood. It was reported that he shot himself through the heart. A suicide note remained, as did an unfinished poem. The newspapers also reported that Polonskaya was married, but unwilling to leave her husband. The officials deemed it a suicide. A lover's quarrel.

Soon after, an investigating police officer discovered that the bullet that had penetrated Mayakovsky's heart was of a different calibre than the revolver found in the dead poet's hand. And while it was reported that he had shot himself once in the heart, neighbours reported hearing two shots. The investigating police officer, an experienced detective, began by taking photographs, studying traces from the gunshot on Mayakovsky's shirt, recording the pattern of blood on the carpet on which Mayakovsky fell. He checked the authenticity of the suicide note. The possibility of a forgery was suggested, but detailed handwriting analysis revealed the suicide note was genuine even though it indicated a psycho-physiological state of agitation. To complicate matters, within ten days, the officer investigating Mayakovsky's suicide was shot to death by an unknown assailant. The case was promptly closed. A mass public funeral was arranged by the state in the wake of Mayakovsky's passing.

In his poem, 'Cloud in Trousers', Mayakovsky asked if people could turn themselves inside out. He felt that the world had been conquered by materialism. He was a Futurist, a poet, a playwright, a rebel. Madness was his greatest attribute. But the hero of 'A Cloud in Trousers' was haunted by the very thought of insane asylums. Insanity recurs throughout the author's work. Despite this, Mayakovsky's close friends felt that the investigation into his death was a cover-up, a slap in the face to justice. Others felt that the government had politically pressured the writer, leaving suicide as his only option. Regardless of such speculations, Mayakovsky's body was buried at the Moscow Novodevichy Cemetery. The funeral was attended by over 150,000 mourners, a number exceeded only at the funerals of Lenin and Stalin. His brain was immediately taken for examination at the Moscow Brain Institute.

The Moscow Brain Institute originated when German physician Oskar Vogt was one of several neurophysiologists consulted on Lenin's illness, which later turned out to be a brain hemorrhage, and following the Soviet leader's death, he was granted the brain for histological study. Vogt discovered that Lenin's brain contained extraordinary numbers of 'giant cells', which he believed indicated superior mental function. In 1925, Vogt accepted an invitation to establish an Institute for brain research in Moscow under the auspices of the nation's Health Ministry. While in Germany, Vogt and his wife, Cécile Vogt-

Mugnier, were friends with and received funding from the Krupp family, one of the key manufacturers of steel, artillery, ammunition and armaments during the First and Second World Wars. Cécile's research into brain cell functions through her cytoarchitectonic examinations sometimes went beyond Oskar's. She excelled in the study of the physiological properties, metabolic processes, signalling pathways, life cycles, chemical compositions and interactions of brain cells. In their research, Vogt-Mugnier and her husband focused on identifying functions in the neocortex, part of the mammalian brain that deals with higher-order operations including cognition, sensory perception, physical motor commands, spatial reasoning, language and sex. It is difficult to say how many of these functions were illuminated through dissections of grey matter that once belonged to notable individuals.

On the day of Mayakovsky's death, when Yuri Olesha, Veronika Polonskaya, Mikhail Yanshin, and other friends and acquaintances sat waiting in the parlour, the doctor in question swiftly emerged from the bedroom, muttered something, marched past them, leapt into a waiting vehicle and whisked Mayakovsky's brain away to Room 19 of the Moscow Brain Institute. Wax models of famous brains are available for viewing by those fortunate enough to gain access to the Institute. The television program I watched while eating breakfast explained that the brains are marinated in formaldehyde until they are ready to be dissected, at which point they are frozen in liquid nitrogen and sliced with blades as thin as one micron. The layers are coated with a special gold solution and pressed between delicate glass microscope slides. Gold. The 79th element. 79, a natural number, a prime number. Diviners say that whenever the number 79 appears, then angels are prompting you to follow your instincts. Room 19. 19 is a natural number and a prime.

19 is a combination of the first and last single digit numbers.
1 and 9. Alpha and Omega.

Once obtained, Mayakovsky's brain was prepared, carefully
sliced, and studied under electron-microscopes. Microscopic
photographs were taken and archived. Gold reacts with photons
bombarded through electron-microscopes, permitting views of
irregularities, tiny creases in brain tissue where thoughts once
flew—troughs, rivulets, gorges, ranges, a topography of mind. It
is uncertain whether these examinations could reveal echoes of
the 18th Brumaire, the siege of Leningrad, the fragrance of fresh
grain, an aria from *La Bohème*, a beckoning blue sky, sparrows
winging overhead, or cranes, perhaps, frozen in time under the
microscopic gold, wing-shapes forming letters across the blue
dome of a cloudless sky. Unreadable words set against a rose-
gold sunrise, emerging dew on tall grass marked by an ornitho-
logical clocking of time. At break of dawn, only periodic chirps
of birds separated by moments of stillness stretching over the
glass lake, the sun's warmth, and then, a gradually growing cas-
cade of songbirds, layered atop each other, each timed perfectly
to their moment during the sun's rise, the concert beginning in
near darkness. Such might be the microscopic gold-dust readings, sequestered within fragile sheets of laboratory slides. The
brain, finely split, layered and sandwiched between delicate
glass plates. The plates softly wrapped, tucked and locked inside
dark silk-lined boxes for future study. Mayakovksy's brain was
only one of many collected in Room 19 of the Institute.

Sakharov's brain was the most recent significant addition to
Room 19. Sakharov designed the Soviet Union's RDS-37 system, a code name for thermonuclear weapons. He was the father
of the Soviet nuclear bomb. A genius, who, like Einstein, had
misgivings, pangs of guilt, became a social critic, turned against
the system. Sakharov was arrested on January 22, 1980,

following his public protests against Soviet interventions in Afghanistan. He was sent to internal exile in the city of Gorky. During the Second World War, Gorky was the primary supplier of military weaponry to the Eastern Front. Following the war, the city was declared 'closed', and no foreigners were permitted visits. In Gorky, Sakharov found himself cut off from contact with friends and colleagues. He endured ongoing harassment by the secret police.

While exiled in Gorky, Sakharov continued research and activism. When he became fixated on a problem, he would forget to eat. One day in Gorky, he forgot breakfast and instead wrote a letter to a fellow physicist encouraging him to continue his human rights activism. I read somewhere that in his letter, Sakharov said, 'Fortunately, the future is unpredictable, and because of quantum effects, uncertain.' He maintained that the U.S. military-industrial complex and KGB-inspired militarism were both gaining strength, threatening the stability of the entire world. Super-militarization was consuming all available resources. An indeterminate future supported his convictions. In 1971, he sent a telegram to the Soviet Ministry of Health demanding a halt to compulsory therapeutic treatment using medications injurious to the mental activity of political prisoners. Later, he went on hunger strikes to draw attention to continued threats against him and his family. Such actions did little to ingratiate him with the Soviet politburo.

When he was nominated for the Nobel Peace Prize, Sakharov was refused permission to travel to Oslo to receive the award. Instead, his wife, Elena, read his speech at the ceremony. On December 10th, moments before reading her husband's Nobel speech, Elena Bonner stated that Sakharov was part of a group that for two days had been standing in the cold, outside the court building in Vilnius, Lithuania, awaiting the sentencing of Sergei Kovalyev, imprisoned for anti-Soviet agitation and propaganda arising from his Samizdat human rights bulletins. Sakharov's Nobel acceptance speech was titled 'Peace, Progress, and Human Rights'. He called for an end to the arms race, raised concerns for the environment, encouraged international cooperation, and demanded respect for human rights. He declared that he was sharing his Nobel Prize with political prisoners of conscience, including Kovalyev. Among bureau chiefs in Moscow, sympathy for Sakharov's views underwent a meteoric crash.

Tolerance for his activism hit ground zero shortly after 1974 when he was awarded the Prix Mondial Cino Del Duca, a prize for those whose scientific or literary work forwards a message of modern humanism. Others awarded the Prix include Jorge Luis Borges, Václav Havel, Milan Kundera, Jean Anouilh, Ernst Jünger and William Styron. In 1976, Yuri Andropov, head of the KGB, declared Sakharov 'Domestic Enemy Number One' before an assembly of high-ranking KGB officers. However, the quantum effects of uncertainty shifted the political stage, and in December 1986, Gorbachev released Sakharov from exile. For a while, with Perestroika and Glasnost, the doors of perception shifted, opening to a different view. But, more recently, the drive to arms has reasserted itself.

As I watched the PBS program on television, it occurred to me that we fetishize great minds, or the brains of great minds. I wondered how the passions of either Sakharov or Mayakovsky might appear under an electron microscope. I kept watching the television documentary about the Brain Institute. On December 14, 1989, Sakharov retired to his study for a nap. He was to present an important speech the next day before the Congress in Moscow. When she went to waken him, Elena found him dead on the floor. Although he was later interred in the Vostryakovskoye cemetery in Moscow, it only took a short while for the 'fast reaction team' to arrive, remove Sakharov's brain, and safely whisk it away to Room 19. Some say that this act was accomplished without permission, and the de-braining happened a short twenty minutes before his death was announced on Moscow radio and television. Unsettling mysteries remain. Sakharov's brain was considered the last important addition to the Moscow Brain Institute, a link between the past and present symbolizing a reputation for ideological revisionism.

As it progressed, the TV program revealed arguments among Institute staff concerning whose brains they were working on. The camera crew interviewed several workers but found discrepancies unapparent to some who had worked in Room 19 for years. Katya was the first. Wearing a white lab coat, she was youngish, haggard, but clearly experienced. She spoke from her work station, explaining that she did the slicing and preparing of Sakharov's brain, maintaining that she'd worked on it for over two years. She said that she admired Sakharov and was proud to be trusted with this important addition to the Institute. The film crew shifted positions and learned from Natali and Ivan that Katya was labouring under a misconception. *They* were the senior members of the team. Both were partly greying, slightly overweight, and clearly secure in their positions. Katya had only been with the Institute for seven years. Ivan and Natali had served there from the early days, although neither was there years ago, when Mayakovsky's brain arrived. They explained that it was necessary to keep Katya in the dark as to whose brain she was working on. Investigations were secretive. New staff members functioned strictly on a need-to-know basis, and were told only enough to carry out their tasks. When pressed, neither Natali nor Ivan could confirm or deny the identity of the brain that Katya was working on. Natali quietly explained, off record, that Katya was, is in fact, working on a fragment of Lenin's brain, but as leader of the investigating team, she was not permitted to reveal this to anyone, not even Ivan, even though she and Ivan had laboured together for over twenty-three years. Of course, following political revisionism, this knowledge could now go public, all in the spirit of reform.

But, Ivan disagreed, explaining that he was visited by members of a secret sub-committee who informed him that he was only to work on a comparative study of Mayakovsky's and Sakharov's brains, looking for similar patterns that might explain 'deviant' behaviour. The slices were to be compared side by side, layer by micro-thin layer, until the secrets of both brains were disclosed under the electron microscopes.

A micron is a unit of measurement equivalent to one thousandth of a millimetre. An electron microscope can easily detect irregularities in surfaces that are only a millimicron or one thousandth of a thousandth of a millimetre in thickness. A micro-millimetre. The common factor was gold. Gold has an atomic mass of 196.96654. Gold atoms could easily be separated by a nuclear blast. During the 1950s, atomic bomb tests were conducted in the Steppe region of northeast Kazakhstan. In 1948, Sakharov's secret study group at FIAN, the Physical Institute of the Academy of Science, realized that they could add a shell of natural, unenriched uranium around a core of deuterium, thereby increasing the overall yield of their nuclear device. The uranium would capture neutrons and generate fission as part of the thermonuclear chain-reaction. This idea of a layered fission-fusion-fission bomb led Sakharov to call it the *Sloika*, or layer cake. It is unknown whether the concept of a layer cake was ever detected under the special gold solution.

One of the younger workers in Room 19 is Dzintra, whose name means 'amber', which has the connotation of clarity.

Amber is fossilized resin from evergreen trees and is treated as a gemstone. This gold-coloured gem is considered to be a soothing restorative. Dzintra is a Latvian-born electron-microscopist who informs the camera crew that she is pleased that the Baltic States achieved independence from the Soviet Union in 1991. Dzintra has been working ten-hour shifts at the Institute for over five years. She has layers of slides stacked before her. When asked about the brains of Sakharov and Mayakovsky, she says that once upon a time there were many thin sheets of glass stored in individual boxes with silk linings. But then, they became the subject of intense comparative study. Hundreds of sheets are required when dissecting a single brain, and many comparative studies of different brains at the Institute have been conducted. She comments that there are only fifty-two playing cards in a deck, not counting the jokers. For all she knows, the brains of Mayakovsky, Lenin, Stalin, Gorky and Sakharov have been shuffled together like a deck of cards. A layer cake. Dzintra's comments closed the television program, leaving me shuffling uncertainties and an indeterminate future.

I wondered what Dzintra might have discovered upon examining Mayakovsky's brain. What might the cytoarchitectonic topography reveal under an electron microscope? With the full brunt of science pushing for a revelation, might some deviant pattern emerge? Could the golden glow of the electron beam illuminate a link between science and the ephemeral? Might science displace the Roma woman's divination? I am returned to the moment of Mayakovsky's death. Following the astounding split second of the bullet's entry, might the electron microscope serve as eyewitness to the passion of two bodies, lips locked, arms entwined, only to unfold them, map-like? What neurons? What cellular interactions? The olfactory senses are wired to memory function. Can tectonic ridges inside the glass plates trace the sound of smoke drifting from a summer camp-fire, a field of fresh wildflowers basking in morning sun, moon-light penetrating crisp, pungent pine, soft moss underfoot, the perfume of enthrallment, the honeydew of another's lips, cordite from a pistol shot, a surge of antimony, barium, and lead from the volley? At that moment, what clouds, what lake, what crys-tals of ice form over the glassy surface? The scratch of a pen on paper, a blood-flower exiting the heart. Valleys are mountains seen from the other side. Deserts are oceans. The sound of the bullet tearing flesh, the self, a naked dream dancing on a clock. Eyesight fails, blood's blossom expands on thin carpet, body atoms shut down, each a dying star, a light extinguished, alone at last, the final utterance, an apostrophe.

I cannot know what Dzintra discovered. But I can tell you what the Roma diviner saw, whispered from palm to palm, passed from time to time, a gift to my mother, who learned from her and shared with me. This is what arrived in my hand. The diviner saw beyond what appeared in the newspapers. She saw the revolution, saw a young actress in love with a wild-eyed poet. Saw the poet, a confirmed communist, his meteoric pas-sion burning reason into madness, crashing, swallowed in a sea of letters. He doted, wrote poems. The actress, flattered, knew they had no future, and instead chose safe domesticity and social status by marrying another, a fellow actor, a director. But she carried on the affair. The poet hoped to draw her into his bohemian life. She was charmed. He insisted she abandon the marriage, manoeuvred to steal her love. She resisted. He threat-ened suicide, or to kill her if she refused him. She had to break things off. Her husband, an open-minded revolutionary, under-stood how conventions of marriage were transformed by upheaval, but this was too much. He ventured to extricate her from a quagmire of pointless passion. They visited the poet's flat, to talk. As a precaution, the director gave the actress his pistol, knowing only too well the vicissitudes of the mad poet. Upon arrival, the poet was shocked to see the husband, recognized him from stage and screen. The poet insisted on speaking to the actress alone, in his bedroom. The actress agreed. The husband, a man of reason, acquiesced. Sequestered in the bedroom, the actress and poet argued. He again threatened suicide. His eyes ablaze, the suicide note on the writing table, he brandished his revolver at himself, then her. Violently slammed his open palm atop the writing table. Grabbed her shoulder. She panicked, reflexively pulled her husband's pistol from her purse. The weapon discharged, piercing the poet's heart. He collapsed beside his bed. Collapsed onto the worn carpet, his unused revolver still in hand. She screamed. Her husband entered. Saw what happened. Knew what to do. A playhouse director. He staged the scene. Seized the bedcover and sheets, threw them back. Seized the poet's still warm hand and forced it to fire one round into the mattress, the revolver remained in the poet's hand. The naked mattress swallowed the bullet. The director restored the sheets, the bedcover. Left the body where it was lying on the floor. Grabbed the actress. Pulled her through the front door. Abandoned the blood-soaked body by the bed. Drawn by the noise, a neighbour appeared at the entrance to her next-door flat. Asked about the noise. They said they were just leaving and heard a shot. They hurried back into the flat, 'found' the poet on the floor, life ebbing, suicide note on his writing table. Then, they called the authorities, called friends. This is where the story begins.

THE RAZOR'S EDGE

Autumn, 1944. I am walking across the cobblestones of the town square in Riga. A foreign power has occupied the country. Armoured vehicles and uniformed soldiers abound. I watch a squad of soldiers flatten six male and two female guerilla fighters against a stone wall. A man walking next to me whispers that they were among the *mežabrāļi*, the forest brothers' resistance. A firing squad has assembled. It is a clear-sky day. I try to walk lightly past the fighters about to be executed. Two soldiers grab my arms from behind, and half-carry and half-drag me to the same stone wall. The man who was walking next to me, who just whispered to me, watches in disbelief. Within seconds two more soldiers seize him the same way. A small group of stragglers gather to watch. The two of us are shoved against the wall. The resistance fighters sing four lines of a traditional folk song, and when done shout 'Klip, klap, klap'. The soldiers are unaware of the song's cultural legacy, or its reference to water mills or windmills. Nor are they aware of the allusion to a circular folk dance where everyone holds hands.

The two soldiers who seized me push my shoulders into the wall and drape a cloth bag over my head. Two other soldiers do the same to the man who was seized a moment after me. The resistance fighters already had bags shoved over their heads by the time I was pushed against the wall. I listen as the soldiers' boots trudge away. I am one of ten against the wall. I remember seeing as many soldiers in the firing squad. I remember as we were lined up, an officer barked orders in a language that I didn't understand. Before I was bagged, I watched the soldiers load cartridges. Silence. A pause. Then, the command. Rapid non-stop single-action rifle fire follows. A bullet buzzes past my ear. A stone chip strikes the back of my neck. I wait, wondering where a bullet will hit. Gut, heart, brain? If brain, that would be easy. Lights out. The rifles keep firing, but I don't get hit. I imagine some strange force, some invisible energy bubble emanating from my body, deflecting the bullets, but it can't last. I imagine the dark that will follow. These thoughts occur in a split second but feel like an eternity. The rifle fire stops abruptly. We are ordered to remove the bags over our heads. The firing squad has shot over our heads. A warning to me and the man who whispered to me. A warning to the small group of stragglers who gathered to watch. The soldiers drag the resistance fighters away for 'interrogation'. I watch as the soldiers use their rifle butts to clip the heads of several resistance fighters. They depart wordlessly, leaving me and the other man at the wall. He has fainted, and now lies on the ground in a puddle of his own urine. We were, I was, released, with nowhere to go. This is a recurring dream. I awake to darkness.

———

This morning, I stepped out of the shower, looked in the bathroom mirror and felt an uneasy spirit move me. Mirrors trouble me. I remember mirrors when I interviewed Julia Kristeva in Toronto. She waltzed out of the elevator of an upscale Toronto hotel, a large goblet of Shiraz in hand. The hotel lobby was lined with enormous mirrors that reflected her pirouette. She said, 'I know in Canada, we must not drink alcohol on the elevator, but I … I am Julia Kristeva!' With that, we moved to the bar for an interview. She spoke about *The Samurai*. Her novel traced the life of Olga, a young Eastern European woman and her intellectual friends who were based on writers and theorists from the *Tel Quel* group, including Sollers, Levi-Strauss, Lacan and Cixous, among others. A *roman à clef*. Olga's group travelled from 1960s Paris to Maoist China, then to New York, and back to Paris. The plot engages Asian notions of Samurai culture. I mentioned that as an advanced martial artist, I embraced the aesthetics and discipline that unite mind/body/spirit. She elaborated, saying that, for a true martial-artist, life always involves a race against death and paradoxically, towards death.

This morning, I gazed in the mirror, noting that I was due for a haircut. I recalled Lacan's words on the split resulting from a misrecognition of the self during the 'mirror-stage'. He said the unconscious is structured like a language. I know that images are also language. Whenever I see myself in a mirror, I grow uncomfortable with my self slipping beneath my image. The submergence of the signified beneath the signifier. Sometimes, I wonder what my *imago*, my mirror 'other', thinks. I'm perturbed by the loop of language, how it keeps pointing back at me, at my desires. I recall talking with Kristeva about the sash of desire, how we're bound by our own words, our own thoughts. She said that one goal of a Samurai is to cut through that sash, cut through the knot of language. I noticed that someone at the bar was leaning in, eavesdropping while she explained how Mandarins were people of power and authority, and how Samurai were greater because they had abandoned materiality, and had no aspiration to be masters. I wondered what the eavesdropper thought. Then, she talked about the struggle of facing an absence at the core of being. She recalled Celine who said we are all on a personal journey 'to the end of the night'.

This morning, my *imago* mocked me. I ignored it. Instead, I checked my email. I got a message from Alan, my pal in Montreal. He attached an article by Anthony Bourdain, the New York chef who travelled the world, working his way up from kitchen helper to internationally celebrated super-chef. It was an older article titled, 'Don't Eat before Reading This', published in the *New Yorker*, April 1999. Bourdain was spilling the beans about what happens in fancy kitchens and restaurants.

Alan, a punk-rocker, is an impresario who organized a music and writing fest in Montreal, years ago. He brought in talents like Burroughs, Acker, Huncke, and Giorno. He's in remission from cancer and likes to remind me of Burroughs's 'intersecting lines', a synchronicity that sometimes spontaneously happens. I met Burroughs in Toronto when I was editing my literary magazine. His shotgun paintings were part of a touring show presented by Montreal's Oboro gallery. The Toronto show happened downtown in '89 at the Cold City Gallery. Burroughs walked in and said, 'I want a vodka and a Chesterfield, and I don't mean a place to sit down.' I used a pair of his shotgun paintings for the front and back cover of the 10th anniversary issue of my lit mag. James Grauerholz handled the details. It was around that time that Alan invited me to read in Montreal. He booked funky nightclubs like *Foufounes Electriques*. I appeared onstage the same night as John Giorno and Herbert Huncke. Huncke was a dyed-in-the-wool Beat. Giorno and his band were super-punks. Later, we all drank vodka late into the night.

Since then, I've moved south to Windsor. The St. Clair River mirrors the Detroit skyline each day I drive by. I think of Motown, the big three automakers, Aretha Franklin, Nine Mile. Sitting at my computer this morning, I read Alan's email and Bourdain's *New Yorker* article.

Bourdain's friends called him 'Tony'. There was a follow-up article by Marky Ramone, who called Bourdain a 'true punk'. It's funny how 'punk' used to be an insult, but now it's a compliment. Poet. Bad boy. Renegade. Outsider. Wild one. Mensch. Tony and Marky met at restaurants in New York to discuss cooking and music. Marky's grandfather was a chef at the Copacabana and the 21 Club during the '40s and '50s. Bourdain hung out at CBGB's in the '70s, and dedicated his book *Nasty Bits* to the Ramones. He'd host musicians at his uptown restaurant, Brasserie Les Halles. Marky remembered how they'd talk about different groups including the Voidoids, Johnny Thunders and the Heartbreakers, the Dolls, the Ramones, Blondie, the Pistols. They were beer and tattoo punk comrades. Tony despised right-wing, conservative fanaticism. I thought about all of this on the heels of an election in Ontario with ongoing debates over the environment, carbon tax, safe injection sites, sex education, medical care, economic tariffs and immigration policy. I remember Bourdain's words on politics. He said that the best revolutionaries were martyrs who died before they could turn into revolting, self-serving, corrupt pieces of crap.

I found Bourdain's article simultaneously hilarious and horrifying. Later that day, I heard of his suicide. Since then, I've learned that in 2009, during the fifth season of his television show *No Reservations*, Bourdain commented on the painful story of his life and how his questionable career ended up as five episodes of a sitcom on the Fox network. He said that, at the end of those episodes, he considered hanging himself in a hotel shower. He spent a lot of time in hotels, had nightmares of wandering hallways with no way out. I have recurring nightmares where I'm trapped in a hotel bathroom, facing a mirror image that isn't me. In his *New Yorker* article, Bourdain explained how chefs and kitchen workers are modern-day Samurai, warriors of a sort, and commented on pains arising from gastronomy. I have worked in fancy kitchens and I can confirm that professional cooks belong to a secret guild whose rituals derive from stoicism in the face of humiliation, injury, fatigue and illness. I've watched kitchen workers confined for endless hours in sweltering, airless spaces ruled by despots. I've noticed that kitchen workers are a superstitious bunch, who remain loyal to their own kind but are contemptuous of outsiders. Bourdain's words about determination and gastronomy made me think of Kristeva, and how Samurai race towards the end of night. Bourdain's 'race' returned him to a time before words. Food itself is a kind of language. In keeping with the Samurai tradition, Bourdain defended the meek. When a Colorado bakery refused to prepare a wedding cake for a gay couple, Bourdain went public, advocating on behalf of the LGBT+ community, arguing that cakes were not protected by the first amendment, nor did the bakers have a constitutional right to discriminate against same-sex customers. In other cases, when faced with anti-pink perspectives, he conceded people had a right to say what they believed, adding that he was offended by stupidly offensive crap with which he disagreed.

I laughed at Bourdain's candid bean-spilling. All of this made sense to me. My mother worked her way up in the Toronto restaurant scene. She started as an independent caterer. I'm not sure why she pursued a career in food. Maybe because she was a World War II refugee and there was never enough to eat. She started at the Wedgewood Restaurant in Toronto's west end, then Julia Child's downtown, and finally ended up managing La Grotta, a high-toned Italian dining establishment in Toronto's core. It no longer exists. I worked as a busboy there. Thinking back, the things Tony said were true. Action in the kitchen was gritty and rough. It was another culture. The kitchen crew had cuts and burns on their hands and wrists, sometimes they drank the restaurant's booze on the side. They ate as they worked while the chef shouted orders amidst ghoulish jokes about cooking them as an entrée if they didn't get in gear.

For my mother, it was a rough ride. She'd go to work early, come home late. Drink too much coffee and sometimes she drank grasshoppers just to keep moving. While bussing tables, I'd hear the crew yelling in the kitchen. Yelling about how food was prepared, how long it took, how it was served, yelling about the produce. All that chaos led to her first heart attack. She switched to real estate afterwards. It was around that time that my father had to take work up north. She became forlorn. My father drove the long road north because he could get work there. He sent home regular cheques, but could only visit every other week. Distances brought fractures.

On finding success through a series of television shows, Bourdain found that constantly being on the road generated loneliness and depression. He'd find himself in an airport ordering a hamburger which wasn't very good, and he'd look at it and think about his TV shows and his life, and he'd begin a downward spiral. When I bussed tables at La Grotta, the place was patronized by local politicos and big-name profs from the university. City councillors like Joe Piccininni, and gurus like Marshall McLuhan. I met Piccininni, and years later studied with McLuhan. They were very successful but didn't seem especially contented. The owner of the restaurant appointed himself my 'godfather', and asked me to call him 'Uncle Sam'. One time, he took me to lunch at another ritzy Italian place. He asked me about my future, if I wanted to work for him, make big money. He had started from scratch and by now had built a law firm, an insurance company and a real estate agency. He was a war refugee too. Another DP. I asked him if money made him happy. He paused a long time, smoked his cigar, looked me in the eye and said, no. So, I stuck to writing and publishing.

Once, I took a friend to La Grotta for lunch. I introduced him to the chef, who remembered my mother and how she used to run the place before the heart attack, and he remembered me, when I was a busboy. That chef made the best *Veal Scaloppini a la Marsala* in town. My friend and I drank Negronis. We drank and ate and talked about the suicide of David Foster Wallace, one of my magazine's authors. Wallace had sent me a hunk of *Infinite Jest* before he published it in '96. Some call it hallucinogenic stream-of-consciousness stuff. For me, it was basic reality. Straight up. But, at 46, he hanged himself. Absence is always present. Afterwards, my friend suggested that next time, we should go to a Korean restaurant on Dundas Street.

I finished the *New Yorker* article, ignored breakfast and went for a haircut. I patronize a chain haircut place called 'The Razor's Edge'. It's an okay place, but I go because of the name. *The Razor's Edge* is the title of AC/DC's twelfth album, which includes a heavy-metal song about living on the edge. The piece sounds like it should be played at maximum decibels and is based on an old farmer's saying about having a very good day, but knowing that things could turn any time. Those farmers knew they were living on a razor's edge. Some music critics think the song is about imminent nuclear annihilation. Maybe so. It reached #2 in the U.S., and #4 in the U.K. It's also the name of two different movies based on a novel by William Somerset Maugham. The first film came out in 1946, starring Tyrone Power. The second, in 1984, starred Bill Murray. The novel is set in Chicago, Paris and India during the 1920s and '30s. It examines divergences between Western materialism and Eastern spirituality. The focus is on Larry Darrell, back from serving as a World War I aviator. He rejects his prewar values, wants to eliminate evil in the world, disregards his fiancée, the status-seeking Isabel Bradley (played by Gene Tierney), spends five years in

India searching for the meaning of life, but finds no answers. The novel's title is drawn from the *Katha Upanishad*, 'The sharp edge of a razor is difficult to pass over; thus, the wise say the path to salvation is hard.' I considered the idea of the dharma, and whether the clarity of Buddhist perception can decipher one's mirrored *imago*. I saw no clear answer. In 'The Pervert's Guide to Cinema', Slavoj Zizek remains silent on *The Razor's Edge*. Other critics were more vocal. The first film was nominated for four Academy Awards, including Best Motion Picture. Anne Baxter won Best Actress in her Supporting Role. For several weeks, Baxter left the set for personal reasons but upon return felt like an outsider because the rest of the cast had already worked out their relationships. Baxter took advantage of being an outsider. Her character Sophie feels like a social outcast who is unable to cope with the loss of her husband and child. The second version of the film was not well received. One critic complained about Bill Murray's portrayal of the leading man, saying, he 'plays the hero as if fate is a comedian and he is the straight man.' But for me, if a Samurai is racing towards some personal night, then that acting approach makes sense. It makes perfect sense.

Specialists say the suicide of fashionista Kate Spade may have triggered Bourdain's decision to quit life. They say suicides lead to other suicides. Like Bourdain, Spade battled demons throughout her life, suffered from anxiety. She hanged herself in her Manhattan apartment. Her husband, Andy, called her the kindest person he knew. Depression doesn't discriminate. I remember once, after an exam at the university where I served, a kid was sitting on the hallway floor just outside an examination room. He was against the wall, leaning over, head in hands. I asked him if he was okay. I asked him if there was something I could do. He said, 'Yeah. No. I'm okay.' Then, he got up and walked away. I recognized him a couple of years later at a graduation ceremony. He came up to me and said I'd saved his life. I asked him what he meant. He said, 'The last time you saw me, I knew I'd flunked my exam. I was going to kill myself, but I said to myself, if even one person comes up and takes the trouble to ask me how I'm doing, then I won't do it. And then, you talked to me.'

Sometimes, there are days when I see something, but I don't do anything. Other times, I react. But sometimes, I don't say anything because it's not my business, or I don't want to interfere or blunder into something that I don't understand. It's a razor's edge between doing something, doing nothing. Bourdain talked about his ups and downs. He spoke of becoming a traitor to his craft, recalling one time when he tried to run a high-profile restaurant in the Times Square area while it was going out of business. Apparently, without telling the chef, the owner had arranged a pre-recorded telephone message advising customers seeking reservations that the doors had closed. All this, despite the kitchen crew's heroic efforts to keep the place afloat.

I stood at the counter of the Razor's Edge. A woman came up and asked how she could help. I told her, 'I'd like a haircut.' She said nothing, stared at her computer monitor for a while, typed something on the keyboard and then said, 'Okay, come with me.' There were only two women working that day. I always get the impression that people working in that salon are only there for interim jobs, and they have greater things planned. There are sixteen chairs set in two rows of eight running the length of the salon. The two rows are divided by large upright mirrors with gaps between them. When getting a haircut, you can see through the gaps between the mirrors. It's strange to see yourself reflected, with a glimpse of someone slipping past on the other side of the mirrors. Sometimes, the person walking by seems familiar. It's hard to tell because the gaps between the mirrors are narrow, and you only catch a *shufti*, a glance. The hairdresser took me to the last chair at the end of the right row. She draped a cloth over my head and around my neck, pushed my shoulders into the chair. She asked what I'd like. I told her. She nodded, loaded the trimmer cartridge onto the cutter, and said, 'You ever heard of Anthony Bourdain?' I was going to say no, because I wasn't interested in talking, but I'd just read that *New Yorker* article, so, I said, yeah, he was a big-time chef and all. And she said, 'Yeah. Well, he's dead, killed himself earlier today. I'm devastated. I was a big fan.'

Then she started talking about Bourdain and how he travelled the world, and how she watched his TV shows. And then, she said, 'You ever heard of Charlie LeDuff?' And I said, 'Yeah, he's that irreverent journalist-author working in Detroit.' I told her I'd heard about LeDuff from my pal Gervais, a journalist with the *Windsor Star*. This warmed her up and she told me how her daughter used to work for that newspaper but now works at the university. While working for the newspaper, her daughter was invited to a press party in Detroit. So her daughter went, and was standing at the bar, and this older guy was standing next to her, and they started chatting. Turns out he was Charlie LeDuff, the guy who wrote *Detroit, An American Autopsy*. He wrote that book when the big three automakers were on the ropes. He introduced himself, and her daughter said, 'Wow, that's great! My mother's a big fan of yours!' And Charlie said, 'Well, phone her up and I'll talk to her right now.' So, the hairdresser told me how her daughter phoned her up and said, 'I'm at that press party in Detroit, and there's someone here who wants to talk to you.' And she put LeDuff on the phone, but he was coy and said, 'I hear you're a fan of Charlie LeDuff?' And the hairdresser told me that she said, 'Yeah, I'm a big fan, I've read his journalistic articles, and I sometimes watch him on TV, and I loved his book on Detroit, and the new book, too, *Shit Show, the Country's Collapsing'*. And when she mentioned LeDuff's newest book, I said that I'd read a hunk of that book too, and it was *true*, the USA *is* a shit show. And she said, 'Yeah, things are really messed up with foreign trade, North Korea, and the G7's in bad shape, too.' She chatted while trimming. I was impressed by how much she knew about economic theory, late capitalism and world politics. She said, 'Those tariffs the U.S. proposed will backfire and hurt their own workers.' And I said, 'It's all too much for me,' and I asked her more about the phone call. And she said that while she spoke to LeDuff, he complained that it's impossible to watch the news anymore because, there's no more real news, just infotainment. Then, she said, 'I can't watch CNN anymore because of that.' She was trimming with the clippers, and she said, 'You ever notice the women on U.S. television? They all look like Barbie dolls. All the same. Tall. Blonde. Not like on Canadian news, like the CBC. Women on Canadian TV look normal. All different body types—tall, short, large, small, dark, light. Normal, y'know?' So, without mentioning Baudrillard and French theory, I talked about how cultural images are all coded, and how socio-politics starts to deal only with hyper-realities, and how the media keep repeating images that literary theorists call *simulacra*. I mentioned how high culture and pop culture are merging during late capitalism. And she said, 'Well, I'm not surprised, because big media features unrealistic gender-biases inspired by some kind of sicko projected mental disorder, and it's everywhere on radio and especially television.' And then she said that some people's questionable opinions are trumping what would normally be justifiable beliefs, and that U.S. television only aims at swaying public perceptions. And she kept clipping. I wanted to add how a Foucauldian genealogy or a straightforward historical analysis would confirm everything she'd just described, but then I thought theory always loops back on itself, so what's the point. Instead, I asked her more about LeDuff.

So, she repeated how at first, Charlie LeDuff pretended to be someone else, and he asked her *why* she liked LeDuff's writing. Then, she told me that she told *him* that LeDuff never pulled any punches about the things he saw. She paused with the clippers, looked me in the mirror and said, 'It was only *then* that the voice on the other end of the phone confessed that *he* was actually Charlie LeDuff.' She told me how *that* made her day. She got all excited talking to him about writing and politics and all. And he asked her if she liked any other writers. And she said she was a huge fan of Anthony Bourdain, and that she had read all his books, including *Medium Raw, No Reservations, Bone in the Throat*, and so on. And Charlie said, have you read any of *my* other books? And she said, sure, I really liked *Work and Other Sins* and *US Guys*. I watched the mirror as she told me all this stuff while she buzz-cut my hair, and I could hear most of what she said, except when she buzzed past my ears. So, then, she recounted how Charlie told her about the time Bourdain visited Detroit. Turns out, LeDuff took Bourdain to a high-toned restaurant, and they ordered a very special soup. Partway through the meal, LeDuff poured his gin and tonic into the soup, picked up the bowl and drank it. Bourdain looked at him and said, 'If I was the chef in this place and I saw you do that, I'd put a fork into your neck.' Or words to that effect. She said talking to Charlie was her fifteen minutes of fame. And then I said, it's hard to tell why Bourdain killed himself. He had it made, but we can't know about such things. And she said, 'Yeah, Bourdain went through rough times—cocaine, heroin, two marriages, poverty, a lot of difficulty and stress.' And then she said, 'He was in Strasbourg,

France. They were recording an episode of his CNN series *Parts Unknown*. He hung himself in his hotel room between shoots.'

———————

As I walked home, I thought about the synchronicity of my Montreal pal sending me Bourdain's *New Yorker* article, the suicide and the hairdresser talking about it all. But it occurred to me that it probably wasn't synchronicity at all. My Montreal friend must've heard about Bourdain before I did, and sent me the article without commenting. When I arrived home, I looked things up, and it seemed to me that Bourdain's TV show *Kitchen Confidential* was a thinly veiled self-portrait. The storyline went like this: During his youth, a chef finds success, but fails due to alcohol abuse, casual sex and drugs. He sobers up, but can only gain employment in seedy theme restaurants. He is unexpectedly offered a chance to serve as head chef at a high-toned New York restaurant but is given only two days to prepare his kitchen and staff, with the expectation that he will draw kudos from over 300 diners, one of whom happens to be the food critic for the *New York Times*. To make things worse, the food critic is one of the chef's former partners, and she despises him. Despite overwhelming odds, he rallies his staff and charges ahead. The first episode aired September 19, 2005.

The news reports on Bourdain said he'd been dating an Italian actress, who said she was devastated by his suicide. In a statement posted on Twitter, the actress recalled the celebrity chef as 'brilliant' and as her 'protector'. Her public statement came hours after she posted a photo on Instagram. In it, she wore a T-shirt with an image of Sid Vicious, one of Bourdain's idols, and the words '*fuck everyone*' on top. She wrote over the image: '*You know who you are.*' That picture was soon deleted. The news report said that the week before, Bourdain bought a

painting titled, '*The sky is falling, I am learning to live with it.*'
He was racing into his personal night. Cooking may have been
his pre-linguistic discourse, but I wondered who truly understood his creations: *choucroute garnie, chengdu,* or *char kway
teow.* Perhaps other polyglot chefs understood, perhaps not. Perhaps the absence of an audience that grasped the subtlety of his
culinary metonymy evolved into a *manque à être,* an absence at
the core of being, that drove him to use the sash from his hotel
bathrobe in a way that was not intended.

———

Before he split, Bourdain wrote comic books which confirm his
Samurai chef attitude. True horror-show stuff. One series was
titled 'Hungry Ghosts'. Each issue included tales about food told
in the tradition of *Hyakum-monogatari Kaidankai,* an ancient
Japanese Samurai storytelling game from the Edo period,
featuring tales of vengeance, ghosts, and the supernatural with a
Buddhist sense of karma woven in. The *Hyakum-monogatari
Kaidankai* have recently regained popularity in Japan with mas-
ter woodblock and painting depictions of *yurei* (ghosts), along
with television shows and anime movies. Interest has grown in
colleges and universities in North America as well. The traditional ritual went as follows: As night fell, three rooms were prepared. The third room would hold 100 lit *andon,* small oil
lamps, or candles. The *andon* were accompanied by a single mirror placed atop a table. Guests assembled in the first of the three
rooms. They took turns recounting *Kaidan,* stories of ghouls or
supernatural monsters. After each tale, the storyteller would go
to the third room, extinguish one *andon,* and look in the mirror
to see if the ghoul or supernatural spirit in their story had pos-
sessed them. Then, they would return to the first room to listen
to the other storytellers. As the stories and the night proceeded,

and as candles were extinguished one by one, the third room grew darker, creating ideal conditions for the evocation of spirits. The second room was deliberately left empty, reserved for visiting entities. As they approached the 99th story, many would hesitate to continue, fearful of supernatural deities they may have summoned. One aim of this game was to frighten a person to death. Food for thought. Some say such ritualistic storytelling opens a window to another world, and once opened, that window can't be closed. The mirror awaits the storyteller. Others say that when there are only a few burning candles remaining, you hear voices murmuring just beyond the light. Some can't shake the uncanny sense of being watched. For the Samurai, this ritual was a test of courage. There is a Japanese nursery song from the 1660s which describes several young Samurai telling tales in this fashion. Upon finishing the hundredth tale, a samurai moves to extinguish the final candle, but he sees the shadow of a large contorted hand descending upon him. A slice of his katana reveals the 'hand' to be nothing more than the shadow of a spider. Bourdain must've heard of these storytelling rituals during his tour of Japan. His shows *Parts Unknown* and *No Reservations* were recorded in Japan, notably with chef Masa Takayama.

Bourdain's comic books are all about food, and they all feature ghostly specters, including cannibalistic ghouls. It is said that if you feel haunted after such a storytelling ritual, then you should bathe or shower with a liberal amount of salt, lavender or sage. You must tell the spirits to depart, for they hold no power over you. Fear breeds its own strength. Some throw it off more easily than others. Some surrender, throw in the towel, hear the bell call 'last round'. Closing time. Wait for the judge's decision. Others trap themselves in pharmaceutical lockdown, cling to rafts or float, shipwrecked, on life's wayward currents. Bitch-slapped by age, sobriety, time, instant karma. Sharks circling.

He haunts me. I see his face rise behind the mirror. Deadman. Chef. Ghoul. Cannibal. Somehow, I understand the craving, the hunger for the chaos of youth. The star-bright muscular sky. Carefree in blue jeans and silk shirts, streetwise, stupid-smart, ignoring tomorrow, riding raging motorcycle streets, endangering self and others, lost, too late for work, too late for home, somehow understanding everything, knowing nothing, dimly sensing that nothing matters or everything matters.

Stepping out of the shower, I sense him in the mirror, in that hotel room. The sash of the bathrobe, the shower nozzle, the halt of oxygen. Cells shutting down one at a time, starting with the toes, each one, a universe, blinking out, nightfall, the hundredth *andon*. I'm in the barber chair. The hairdresser's finished. Dusts me off. Aims a handheld mirror behind my neck. I see her image standing there. The handheld mirror displays the back of my head. I'm simultaneously looking forward, looking backward. A split second. An eternity.

———

If in distress, contact:

The Canada Suicide Prevention Service (CSPS):
  1-833-456-4566

In the United States, the U.S. National Suicide Prevention
  LifeLine: 1-800-273-8255

The International Association for Suicide Prevention
  (IASP): https://www.iasp.info/

Befrienders Worldwide: https://www.befrienders.org/

DON'T TRY TO FIND US: FOUCAULT'S PENDULUM

'There are three stages in the revelation of any truth: in the first it is ridiculed; in the second resisted; in the third it is considered self-evident.' —Arthur Schopenhauer

'The solution to this problem lies in the heart of mankind. If only I had known, I should have become a watchmaker.'
—Albert Einstein

Now, in the month of March, in the year of our plague, I find myself rifling through old papers and file folders. I'm chagrined to find several unpublished reports. One folder covers the uprisings that ignited and blazed through Paris in December of 2019 but subsided with the spread of the global pandemic. By December of 2019, the plague had established itself. Some knew of its existence as far back as November of that year, perhaps earlier. Others predicted such outbreaks years ago. By that December, the contagion had spread in earnest.

Why does December bear such strange fruit? The name implies that it is the tenth month, but it is the twelfth. I checked, and learned that the month's name was retained despite the fact that in 44 BCE, Julius Caesar reformed the ten-month Roman year, to a twelve-month Julian year. Around that time, he was declared *dictator in perpetuum* of the Roman Republic. 'Dictator in perpetuity' is among the titles typically held by Roman emperors. A year later, a group of sixty Roman senators took things into their own hands. They were dubbed 'liberators', but some called them 'serpents' while others called them 'insurrectionists'. They feared that Caesar planned to claim the title of emperor, overthrow the Senate and rule as a tyrant. Some things can be changed. Some things never change. The group was led by Gaius Cassius Longinus, Decimus Junius Brutus Albinus, and Marcus Junius Brutus. Their group stabbed Julius Caesar twenty-three times near the steps adjacent to the Theatre of Pompey. The assassination happened on the 15th day of March, a month named for Mars, god of war, ancestor of the Romans through his sons Romulus and Remus. The 'ides of March' correspond with the 15th day of the month, which is typically illuminated at night by a full moon. It is a time set aside for religious observances, friendly gatherings and it is considered a deadline for settling debts. Today, old friends—and old debts—come to mind.

As I continued rifling through my papers, I found another unpublished report in which I noted that on December 24th, 2006, the massive clock atop the Panthéon building in Paris began to chime. In a time of global pandemic, such occurrences might warrant only a modest mention. But it so happens that the clock had not functioned since the 1960s. To the embarrassment of the clock tower's administrators, somebody had secretly repaired the clock under their noses and then brazenly confessed to that 'criminal act'.

It is morning. I'm half-consciously gazing about my room in the Latin Quarter. Daily flotsam layers various surfaces. A pair of gloves, two hats, a telephone directory, an address book and a large bottle of hand sanitizer that I had the foresight to purchase, perhaps because I'm a neurotic germaphobe akin to Howard Hughes, except that I'm impoverished. When the outbreak began, sanitizer was scarce. The stores were sold out. Those items sat atop my coffee table, including documents about the Panthéon in Paris, along with an older London *Guardian* article, filed under a pseudonym to protect those interviewed. I wondered if such things mattered anymore. Half a year ago, the street outside my room was in a furor. The *gilets jaunes*, the yellow jackets, rallied, only to be met by police wielding water cannons and tear gas. The sounds outside used to awaken me. Now, there's silence and the streets are empty. I slept in. The battery died in my clock radio and the alarm failed. I didn't want to buy a new battery. Infection horrified me. On the table, a TV guide announced yet another biography of Albert Einstein. The tube. The H-bomb. I considered the plague and the bomb and wondered about efficiencies. I've known for years that television 'snow' between channels reveals residual cosmic radiation following the big bang. 'Snow'. Stardust memories after *The Late Late Show*. When asked about the White Sands project, Einstein said: 'The release of atom power has changed everything except our way of thinking, and thus we are being driven unarmed towards a catastrophe. The solution to this problem lies in the heart of mankind. If only I had known, I should have become a watchmaker.' Albert departed ahead of us, cremated, a cloud of ash, and now remains silent. Before his cremation, Einstein's brain was removed by Thomas Stolz Harvey, a pathologist. Questions concerning consent to remove the brain remain unresolved. In 2013, segments went on display at the Mutter Museum in Philadelphia, which exhibited thin slices mounted on slides suitable for cytoarchitectonic analysis using electron microscopes. Some researchers suggest that Einstein's copious *corpus callosum* enhanced interhemispheric communication. Sakharov. Einstein. Brain slides. Electron microscopy. What do they mean? Past, present and future are merely stubborn illusions. Sometimes, there is no return, sometimes there are endless returns. When Sisyphus rolled that rock uphill, it always escaped, and he had to repeat his efforts. Persephone, imprisoned by Hades, the God of the underworld, returned to the surface each spring, thereby renewing life.

Today, I am returned to my second unfiled report wherein I investigated near-forgotten events at the Panthéon. If you take time to look, you can see the Panthéon from the Jardin du Luxembourg, near the Sorbonne. And if you walk south on the left bank of the Seine along Rue Saint-Jacques, you arrive at the 5th arrondissement and Rue Soufflot, normally congested with automobiles and people, full with busy shops and underground parking. But today, nothing. The populace has self-isolated. Not long ago, the street was in half-riot, swarming with yellow jackets and protestors facing off against the gendarmerie. Keep walking eastward and you arrive at Place du Panthéon, perched atop Montagne Sainte-Geneviève. Geneviève, patron saint of Paris. Her feast day, January 3rd, during the first month of the year. Since the French Revolution that former church served as a necropolis; its crypt held the bones of French heroes. From outside, the Panthéon's impressive architecture is punctuated by tall columns that frame the main entrance. Above them rests a frieze with cornice and pediment. Secured atop that, an illustrious dome. The style combines ancient Greek elements with the Gothic, a serene example of neoclassical architecture born during the Enlightenment and meant to inspire trust in a benevolent, orderly government. If you look closely, you might note the optical illusion created by the slight outward curvature of the columns, designed so that the lines look perfectly vertical when viewed at a distance. The dome has three shells, and for full effect, the main facade, with its Corinthian-temple front and sculpture-filled pediment, is best approached by mounting the tall flight of steps on a cool winter day during a light dusting of snow. You should know that the ground deep beneath the building is riddled with tunnels, as is the bedrock beneath much of Paris. Parisians quarried stone for centuries. History sometimes seems incidental, but often betrays desires long hidden.

Here are some of the purported historical 'facts' involving the Panthéon. In 507, Clovis, the first Frankish Merovingian King, chose the site as a basilica to serve as a tomb for himself and his wife, Clothilde. If you're royal, then why settle for a monument when a basilica can be had? Clovis found himself in good company. Soon after, in 512, the patroness of Paris, Sainte-Geneviève, was buried in the same location. Still later, in 1744, after he recovered from a near-fatal illness, Louis XV vowed to erect a church atop the site, to be known as the Abbey Sainte-Geneviève. Near-death experiences among those in power inspire extravagant forms of generosity, particularly when taxes assist with expenses. The architect Germain Soufflot was commissioned to design the abbey. Work began in 1757 and took thirty-four years to complete. Soufflot died before finishing the task. His associate Guillaume Rondelet completed construction in 1791, at the height of the French Revolution. Following the secret flight of the royal family in June of that year, the Assembly of the Revolution chose to transform the church into a civic temple to provide the final resting place for the heroes of the nation. Quatremère de Quincy was given the task of transforming the building into a Panthéon.

With construction completed in 1851, Léon Foucault suspended a twenty-eight-kilogram bob on a sixty-seven-metre wire from the dome of the Panthéon. The bob consisted of a ball of lead covered in brass, and it traced out narrow ellipses, similar to a Spirograph toy. The oscillations of Foucault's pendulum demonstrated the invisible rotation of the earth.

If you walked the streets of Paris a few years ago, then you might have been preoccupied with patrons chatting beneath café awnings or aromas emanating from nearby boulangeries, but you probably would've been oblivious to the fact that you were spinning on the earth's surface at over 800 kilometres per hour.

Back then, if you took time to observe, you might've noted that the plane of Foucault's pendulum swung forward and back, clockwise and in near silence, describing a full rotation in 32.7 hours. The latitude of the Panthéon in Paris is 48 degrees, 52 minutes, north. The planet's bulge affects time itself. If Foucault had placed his pendulum directly over the North Pole, then it would take only one sidereal day for a full rotation. A sidereal rotation is marked by a full transit past the star Aries. Our movements through space and time are almost imperceptible. But sometimes we hold to our myths. Aries is the first sign of the Zodiac, the ram. A ram's Golden Fleece was sought by Jason, and his allies the Argonauts. That story is said to be euhemeristic, based on actual events. The fleece was a symbol of kingship. That object of desire was hung in an oak, at the edge of the known world, protected by a dragon, whose teeth sprouted warriors if planted. That myth oscillates between misfortune and fortune. Adherents to the pendulum theory contend that societies swing from one position to its opposite.

Over time, the Panthéon's purpose swung back and forth. It began as a church, was redesignated as a civic temple. Then it was reinstated as a church. Later, it was redesignated from church to civic temple. Still later, it was declared a church in 1806, only to be returned to a civic function by 1885. Within the Panthéon, there is a large crypt with stone vaults that keep the remains of Voltaire, Victor Hugo, Alexandre Dumas, Marie Curie, Émile Zola, Louis Braille and the Panthéon's designer and architect, Jacques-Germain Soufflot. Recently, French

Holocaust survivor and political activist Simone Weil was interred there. Prior to her, French Resistance fighters Geneviève de Gaulle-Anthonioz and Germaine Tillion joined the shades of earlier French luminaries. From April to October, tourists are typically permitted to enjoy fine views of Paris from the colonnade of the dome. Today, the building is vacant, closed.

In my unfiled report, which I read to a press group years ago but never published, I traced what happened when the Parisian UX (Urban eXperiment) group turned its attention to the Panthéon clock. The UX is the parent organization to a second group of urban guerrillas who call themselves the Untergunther. The Untergunther roam over 200 kilometres of stone tunnels below the city's surface. The group took their name from a song they played as an alarm whenever police approached their clandestine operations. After all, who would play a German song in a Parisian tunnel? That song meant there was little chance of a 'false' alarm. Since then, things have changed. Today, the internet abounds in false reports. I no longer know what is actual, what is mirage. I do know that the UX is clandestine and superbly organized, with some 150 members divided into roughly ten groups. I'm unsure how the pandemic has affected their operations. Before the outbreak of the pandemic, during a covert meeting in an out-of-the-way café, I gathered information by speaking to two UX members. One explained that a group in their organization is all female, a unit of latter-day Persephones specializing in gaining surreptitious access to museums or other institutional buildings after hours. Those adept women memorize the underground mazes from where they carry out their benevolent and clandestine labours. Later, they return to life on the surface. Things have changed since the pandemic.

The Plague of Marseille was among the final outbreaks of the bubonic plague in Europe. It arrived in Marseille in 1720, and in just two years, killed over 100,000 people in the countryside, plus 50,000 in the city. It spread north, taking another 50,000 in the nearby provinces and villages. Given that France had a population of over 20 million at that time, its leaders admitted that the loss was significant, but called it too 'insubstantial' to be alarmed. Nonetheless, the government formed a Conseil de Santé, a Council of Health, which met twice a week at the Louvre in Paris to handle the crisis. In September of 1720, the monarchy of Louis XV appointed Charles Claude Andrault de Langeron as Maréchal and Commander in Chief of the city of Marseille and surrounding regions. His duties included overseeing plague management, distribution of food and relief supplies, destruction of dogs and cats which were thought to be carriers, firing of cannons to dispel 'miasmas', and incineration of any merchandise or property suspected of infection. Many people lost their possessions and livelihoods. Streets, homes and merchandise were disinfected regularly. Maréchal Langeron designated prayer days and organized religious processions, but prohibited all other social events. He ordered the regulation of markets, taverns, inns and brothels. It was a time of martial law. It was a time when the past seemed distant, the present strangely unfamiliar and the future terrifying. It was a time when the Maréchal held absolute power. Due to the extreme measures taken, that plague was contained, but pockets in Paris remained infected. Around that time, because of the plague, or simply because of population growth, many cemeteries in Paris and throughout France were filled to overflowing.

The section of Paris known as Les Halles, less than two kilometres from the Panthéon, is adjacent to Les Innocents, the oldest and largest cemetery in Paris. By the mid-1700s, the cemetery consistently exuded the odour of rotting flesh, and legend has it that perfume shops in Les Halles were forced to relocate to more desirable quarters in Paris. To make matters worse, incessant rains deluged the city in 1780, and with them, the wall around Les Innocents collapsed. Reeking, putrefied corpses spilled from the cemetery into the neighbourhood. A deluge of dead flooded the streets. Consequently, Parisian authorities chose to relocate the dead, and within twelve years, six or seven million were resituated in the labyrinthine tunnels beneath the city's surface. Some of the dead dated back over a millennium, to Merovingian times. Some French Revolutionaries were among those transferred, including Jean-Paul Marat and Maximilien de Robespierre. At first, the remains were placed in haphazard manner, but by the early 1800s, Louis-Étienne Héricart de Thury, director of the Paris Mine Inspection Service, ordered that the underground be arranged as a mausoleum so that the public could visit. He oversaw the neat stacking of millions of human skulls. Similar care was granted to large bones, including femurs arranged into patterns still evident in the catacombs today. Walls of bones now complement large tracts of the underground passageways.

For those who wish to investigate, there's a secret entrance at Denfert-Rochereau. It is aptly named: the corner of fire and stone. But beware. Some have lost their way. And upon exiting, do not go back, search no more. Paris has changed since the 1700s. In old Paris, Rue Saint-Jacques was once a major passage in the Latin Quarter, but it became a laneway after Boulevard Saint-Germain was built as part of Baron Haussmann's Parisian regeneration. Pilgrims commonly travelled along the Chemin de Saint-Jacques-de-Compostelle because it eventually led to Santiago de Compostela in Galicia, Spain, where the remains of the apostle Saint James were said to be buried. Such pilgrims are rare, of late.

It was in 1853 that Napoléon III (Charles Louis Napoléon Bonaparte, nephew of Napoléon I), then Emperor of France, initiated a massive urban renewal project, engaging Baron Georges-Eugène Haussmann to restructure the city with the aim of turning Paris into a modern capital. Haussmann structures are typically six or seven storeys, providing apartments for many, featuring tall airy rooms with windows running from floor to ceiling. Those buildings exude a sense of calm charm that embraces confidence in the foundations of social concord. In such a place, consider late afternoon sun slanting through tall windows, a bottle of Beaujolais, a fresh baguette, green onions, music and your lover. At such times, all's well in the world, apart from the pendulum that slowly swings between harmony and turmoil.

In recent history, there was the rebellion of 1968, with mass protests, demonstrations, civil unrest, a student revolt and a general strike. In 2018, the cry *'aux barricades!'* rose again. It started on November 17, 2018. Mock guillotines appeared in the streets. Unrest began simply with a protest against rising fuel taxes. Those taxes were aimed at reducing dependency on fossil fuels but forsook those relying on ground transport for their jobs. Protests began modestly, with yellow-jacketed individuals obstructing oil-truck traffic at fuel depots. Supermarket entrances were blocked. Drivers were stopped and asked to sign petitions against increased fuel taxes. People were generally supportive. They brought food and drink to the activists. A few weeks into the protests, anger shifted to the president and the French elites. Large-scale riots and urban warfare were met with gendarmes and police in riot gear. Phalanxes of flak-jackets with visored helmets and gas masks shot tear-gas at chanting protesters. The rebellion against carbon taxes metamorphosed into an open revolt against the government and the president. It was said that the 'austerity measures' reduced taxes for portfolios of the wealthy, but raised fees for local services and reduced grants to municipal governments, all while cutting public services. Many declared that the nation was run by a 'president of the rich'. I listened to one yellow-jacket spokesperson declare that two hundred years of universal suffrage had failed, and that voting was a political sham. At a news rally near a barricade, the same activist declared that political impotence is integrated in the constitution which ensures that the people have no actual power. *Some* greens questioned a protest against increased taxes on fossil fuels. *Others* noted that the *gilets jaunes* had successfully exposed the greenwashing of a regressive economic and social agenda. Many joined the fray. New allies included trade unions, farmers upset about reduced prices for produce, students furious about teacher layoffs and increased class sizes. People kept calling the nation's leader a president of the super-rich. Unrest continued. Water cannons and tear gas were turned against the insurgents. Much of the news was not posted outside of France.

Connections become impossible to trace. I know this much. On January 12, 2019, a bakery exploded at the foot of a six-storey Haussmann-style building. The explosion erupted at 6 Rue Trévise at the Boulangerie Hubert, in the 9th arrondissement. A massive pocket of gas accumulated inside the building. Then, it exploded. The blast was heard over a kilometre away. It started a fire that consumed the bakery, most of the ground floor and the apartments above, while setting off alarms, shattering windows and damaging nearby buildings. Fire and ambulance vehicles wailed to the scene. Forty-seven people were injured. At least three died. Reports say the explosion was 'accidental', and no cause was identified. Beatrix, the bakery owner, stood in shock watching the firefighters. She spoke to the news, saying, 'I have no idea what happened. My ovens are electric.' It all started when a fire brigade arrived at 8:37 a.m. to investigate the smell of gas purportedly leaking from an underground source. Insurrection takes many forms. Some seen, others invisible. Nobody knows what happened, nor has a cause been identified. Today, the streets are largely silent.

Several decades ago, the underground tunnels beneath Paris became havens for student and artist groups. Some members of the student groups evolved into the UX. Within the tunnel systems, the UX Persephones worked late nights, silencing alarms to provide group members access to museums, churches and galleries for impromptu artistic and cultural gatherings. Another branch of the UX handled communications, using coded internal message systems and digital radio networks accessible only to members. A third group arranged covert art shows, concerts, literary readings, theatre events and film screenings, often inside public monuments. Raves were arranged in underground quarry sites. A fourth group documented such events using photography or video, while a fifth managed databases of information and oversaw digital technology. Now, it is said that the quarried tunnels are as silent as the bones of the dead that reside there. But that which remains unseen can never be verified.

It is with the sixth UX group that the unseen becomes apparent. Also known as the House of Mouse or the Mouse House, the group specialized in covert restorations of historical sites. I met two members of the group for a brief interview. They wore black clothes, drank black coffee, had a penchant for couscous and, like the rest of the group, had adopted Germanic nicknames. Kunstmann, the art man. Lazar Klausmann, well suited for one who restores or brings things back to life. Lanso, whose name is a triple pun on 'compatriot', 'mercenary' and 'lancer'. Such names resonate with the counterculture of the time, and with the periodical I edited. Because of my own editorial work, I was received as a fellow renegade shit-disturber. I was permitted to share coffee with—what shall I call them? Insurgents? Liberators? They told me their leader was a professional photographer and video editor by day, a quiet woman who oversaw chosen restorations under cover of darkness. They told me that, among other projects, the group had restored an abandoned, historically important 100-year-old government bunker, as well as a twelfth-century crypt holding secrets of the medieval period.

They informed me that one of the first techniques members learn is how to camouflage portals. For example, a short vertical tunnel leading into deeper subterranean passages can be disguised by placing a basin of water fitted to the exact proportions of the tunnel's mouth. Even to a trained eye, the portal appears to be a normal sewer grate filled with grey water that has seeped through the limestone. When one removes the grate, a ladder is revealed leading to a lower level. This ingenuity explains why specially trained police tactical units pursued the UX, but failed to apprehend them.

The Untergunther strive to *preserve* the Parisian heritage, things swallowed by time. In his interview with the London *Guardian*, Klausmann confided: 'We would like to be able to replace the state in the areas it is incompetent, but our means are limited, and we can only do a fraction of what needs to be done. There's so much to do in Paris that we won't manage in our lifetime.' Some measures can be ridiculed, while others are resisted or denied. Some truths remain buried, others become self-evident.

They began in September of 2005. A small group infiltrated the Panthéon. It was near closing time. They permitted themselves to be locked inside. Their mission: to repair the Panthéon clock. The timepiece itself was massive. It's said that it was built and installed in 1850, but precise dates are difficult to verify. It's said that a custodian grew weary of the task of mounting the long staircase to wind the stiff Wagner clock mechanism. The clock hands stopped at ten minutes before 12:00. I can't say if it was before noon or midnight, but the mechanism rested in silence for over forty years until the Untergunther, disgusted by governmental negligence, discovered a side entrance near an unused flight of stairs. Each day, they entered from below and, taking a forgotten flight of service stairs, they eluded the guards. Klausmann observed that opening a lock is an easy thing for a clockmaker. The group worked every night inside the cramped clock chamber atop the building over the next year. They tapped into the electrical grid, connected to computer networks providing specifics regarding clock mechanisms, and established a workshop that included a makeshift table, chairs, hot plate and resource books. It's said that Jean-Baptiste Viot, a professional clockmaker, led the group in painstakingly restoring and cleaning the monumental timepiece. An Untergunther report states that great care was taken to stay true to the heritage of the clock. New parts were installed only when absolutely necessary. After labouring for a year, the task was completed.

The group members debated whether they should inform the Panthéon's officials of their success. They decided to come forward so administrators would know to once again turn the winding mechanism driving the clock. I've heard it said that upon learning of the repair, the astonished chief administrator took a deep breath, then sat down. At first, he thought it was a hoax, but nonetheless chose to advise his superiors. The Centre of National Monuments (CMN), embarrassed by the ease with which they'd been eluded, publicly denied the matter, but privately pressed charges against the vigilantes. An Untergunther press release states that, following the repairs and under cover of a light dusting of snow, the Mouse House cell entered the building and conducted a transmission check. On the night of

December 24, 2006, they wound the clock, rotated the arms and set the correct time. This started the chimes ringing regularly for the next day, discrediting the Centre for National Monuments' attempt to deny the story.

While I cannot verify this, it's reported that, out of spite, the Panthéon's administration secretly recruited an independent company to disable the clock's mechanism. Once again, the arms of the clock stopped moving, but the subterfuge was quickly noticed, making headlines in major newspapers including the London *Times* and the London *Guardian*. The attorney for the Centre for National Monuments demanded the equivalent of 70,000 US dollars to be taken from those who 'tampered' with and 'damaged' the clock by repairing it. His evidence included the fact that a gate lock outside the Panthéon had been broken. In spite of such claims, the chief prosecutor qualified the accusations as 'stupid', noting that all interior locks were intact and that anyone could have damaged the exterior gate. She requested an acquittal. Given that a prestigious national monument had been restored, the president of the tribunal characterized the CMN's accusation as 'absolutely incomprehensible', and although he voiced disapproval of such clandestine operations, he confirmed that all charges would be dropped. Reportedly overwhelmed by the outcome, officials for the Panthéon refused to comment when questioned afterwards by a reporter for *Le Monde*.

As I sat sipping coffee with my two UX interviewees, I was told that the police first encountered the UX in 2004 when they blundered across an underground cinema fully appointed with electricity, security cameras and telephone connections. Rows of carved bedrock provided seats. The underground cavern came complete with bar and couscous stand, tucked inside an abandoned rock quarry 400 metres square and only 18 metres beneath the Eiffel Tower. Apparently, a novice visitor to this UX event had mistakenly identified the couscous machine as a bomb. In a panic, she alerted the authorities. Soon after, a police tactical squad was mobilized using the caller's cell phone as a tracking device. The UX, suddenly alert to the fact that they'd been exposed, cleared out immediately. The police arrived and found only a snow-like dusting of couscous covering the stone ground. There was limited evidence of an underground cinema, a few discarded paper programs. They found the site silent and abandoned, with only a handwritten note saying, 'Do not try to find us.'

Schopenhauer is among those who influenced Camus's *Myth of Sisyphus*, which covers absurdism while swinging between a human need for meaning and the silence of the universe. For his crime of putting Death itself in chains, thereby temporarily preventing anyone on earth from dying, Sisyphus was condemned to endlessly push a boulder up a mountain only to watch it roll down again. For some reason this reminds me of a writer's life. Camus acknowledges Sisyphus's heroics, and states that one ought to imagine Sisyphus happy because his fate was to struggle against the insurmountable. Persephone entered the world of the dead against her will, but once there, oversaw heroes of the underworld. And, she gained an exit for half the year. Though she acts as queen of the stony underworld, with the swing of the annual pendulum, she also serves as a life-giver and fertility goddess of rebirth. It is only Persephone's absence that brings death. Mysteries elude us. What causes movement in the slowly swinging pendulum? Do rewards await in the afterworld? Does a silent universe signify anything?

It's said that the clock atop the Panthéon, final resting place of the heroes of France, rests silently now, subject to the will of administrators accused of sabotaging it a second time. Some things are seen and ridiculed. Others, resisted and denied. Still others seem self-evident. Not long ago, outside my window, I listened to loud protesters, water cannons and shrieking crowds reacting to tear gas canisters. Perhaps spring will bring something new. For now, there is only silence.

POSTLUDE:
THE SOUND OF SMOKE

T oday is the summer solstice, the longest day, the shortest night of the year. Each year, my friends have gathered on this day, to dance and dream, to give thanks and share stories. But this year, I chose to be alone, tracing turbulent absences, and incomplete accounts.

It is late June. There is a joss stick burning atop the small antique writer's desk in my living room adjacent to a hoop of wiingashik, sweetgrass. The smoke rises directly to the great mystery. Words never do justice. I type with a nagging awareness that words are not the things themselves. Only substitutes.

I'm aware that there are two joss sticks, the one in my room, and the one I write about. Still, some things can be said. I can say some things. I can say that the joss stick is a compound of twenty-three herbs gathered from the Himalayan ranges, rolled by hand in keeping with ancient Tibetan ritual. I can say that some of the herbs come from the Silver Valley of Kulu, while others are gathered from the snow-capped mountains surrounding the hill station of Manali in the Himachal Pradesh which stands at an elevation nearly half the height of Everest itself. A joss stick is a joss stick is a joss stick. Fire. Smoke.

Everest. Everest was named after a British knight, a geographer who reputedly never set eyes upon that peak. Local Nepalese and Tibetans called the mountain Kangchenjuga, Dhaulagiri, Deodungha, and Chomolungma. Chomolungma means 'Goddess Mother of the World' or 'Goddess of the Valley'. In the 1960s the local government chose to instate the Sanskrit or Vedic name Sagarmatha, which can be understood as the 'Peak of Heaven' or 'Forehead of the Sky'.

Kangchenjuga, Dhaulagiri, Deodungha, Chomolungma, Sagarmatha is part of the Himalayas which cradle the Gangotri Glacier, which is said to be the source of the sacred Ganges River arising at the confluence of the Bhagirathi and Alaknanda rivers, joining the Dhauliganga, Nandakini, Pindar and Mandakini, among many lesser headstreams, to form one of the largest rivers on the planet. Words. Names. Some seem strange at first, clad in arcane meaning. It is said that to bathe in the Ganges on solstice day brings *dasha-hara*, the cleansing of ten sins, or, some say ten lifetimes of sins. These words and names find roots in ancient Sanskrit, and though they may seem foreign to some, they have a familiar ring to my Baltic ear. It is said that the roots of my language arose from Sanskrit, journeyed through the Hindu Kush, through the Urals and Caucasus, past Greece, heading north by northwest beyond the Pontic steppe.

In my room, a plume of the joss stick's smoke drifts through curved air, a slow-dancing turbulence, a soft chaos. Any history of my ancestral language retraces millennia forgotten by time itself. I can say that this story ends over half a century ago with a slow yet abrupt death, much like incense that burns gradually, but abruptly comes to a stop. There is more to say about multiple meanings, and how the indeterminacies of words affect perception. Meaning folds back upon itself, dispersing and collapsing in the turbulence of discourse, dispute and argument. Uncertainties emerge. Contradictions. The story is complicated by the fact that I don't hold authentic records of all that happened, only a handful of letters sent from a dead uncle in Siberia, along with historical accounts that don't always agree. Language is ineffective in conveying what needs to be said. Unwillingly, I've become part of the story. Questions lie when reconstructing incomplete facts, half-truths, enigmas. What remains is incompletion, interruption. Only the dead know what happened.

Incense snakes through air. I am reading letters sent by my uncle sent to a relative in Riga, who forwarded them to my father in Toronto, who left them to me. When I was young, my reading lessons extended into Latvian and basic Russian. Books sent by another uncle from the old country offered Baltic folk tales translated into the Russian language. My mother insisted I read them. I protested. Why should I learn Latvian or Russian when everybody here speaks English? She always had the same replies. Know your mother tongue. Learn the language of your enemy. During the war, my mother was a refugee but found work as a translator for the Adjutant General's office of the United States. So many languages. So many viewpoints. I was a boy when the Cold War escalated. Intercontinental ballistic missiles. Khrushchev hammering his shoe on the tabletop at the United Nations. Che Guevara and Castro ignited each other, and during the Cuban Missile Crisis questioned Moscow's commitment to transnational socialism. Kennedy warned of dire reprisals. Smoke. Those events hung in the air, assumed an indeterminable form, but always with a degree of predictability. Each day, the *Toronto Star* newspaper featured a sober editorial cartoon depicting the doomsday clock, with caricatures of the leaders of the Soviet Union and the United States. We watched images of mushroom clouds on television. We followed the regimented cliché. In the event of impending nuclear attack, the Dew Line radar system would provide twenty minutes of warning. At school, we were taught to close the curtains, and hide under our desks to avoid splintering glass or falling plaster caused by an H-bomb blast. It wasn't known if taking refuge under desks was adequate protection during a thermonuclear detonation, or if it was simply a capitulation, a protocol, an orderly way to receive death when nothing else could be done. 'Little Boy.' 'Fat Man.' Hiroshima. Nagasaki. We waited stupidly beneath our desks. I could smell floor polish on the linoleum, ink in my inkwell. The graffiti beneath the desk was punctuated with multi-coloured pieces of chewing gum. The city conducted daily air-raid siren tests to ensure readiness. Newspapers were delivered each day, and we'd flip to the editorial page. Each day, the hands on the doomsday clock came one minute closer to midnight. We knew we were going to die.

Today, I am reading the journal of Colin Thubron, a British travel writer who visited the Siberian Gulag camps of Vorkuta and Kolyma. He explained that Kolyma received tens of thousands of prisoners each year. They were shipped in by sea. The port of Magadan was built near Kolyma, along with a road to gold mines where so many perished. He said that the roadway was dubbed the 'Road of Bones', and Kolyma was called 'The Planet' because it was detached from all reality. Moving to another Gulag, Thubron reports that Vorkuta was a place of dread, a site of mass forced labour where tens of thousands endured inhuman conditions. The key purpose was to kill inmates. Winter temperatures dropped to -40 degrees Fahrenheit, blizzards howled, the prisoners (*katorzhane*) lived in lightly boarded tents, with sawdust sprinkled on a floor of moss and permafrost. Prisoners laboured twelve-hour days, hauling coal trucks. Most were broken within three weeks. They became robotic, their grey-yellow faces decorated with ice, blood and frozen tears. When fed, they stood in silence. Some tried to earn more food but the effort was too taxing. Thubron notes that within a year 28,000 prisoners died. Aleksandr Solzhenitsyn wrote of such places and said that prisoners were sometimes locked in isolation cells. Some, deprived of clothing, their bodies collapsed within ten days, within two weeks they died. In July 1953, there was an uprising reacting to the death of Stalin. Prisoners sought release. The Gulag camp administration ignored them. Guards opened fire on the inmates on August 1. According to Solzhenitsyn, 66 people were killed. Medical aid was withheld. Among those shot was the Latvian Catholic priest Jānis Mendriks, nicknamed 'Servant of God'. He was born in Latgale, as was my mother. He continued services among the prisoners secretly and devotedly. Sentenced to ten years of forced labour plus five years in exile. Shot dead at Pit No. 29.

I read Thubron's account in an attempt to map the past. There are other archival documents. Testimonies record the perceptions of prisoners and imprisoners. Fire. Smoke. Views disagree. Forced labour. Corrective labour. Ideologies clash. Contention enters the arena of language. Among Soviets, Gulag camps were described as superior to western penitentiaries. They argued that the emphasis was on 're-educating' prisoners who posed a threat to the motherland. Labour was the instrument of enlightenment. Inmates could emerge as valued citizens of the workers' state. Advocates of the prison system contradict journalists and the accounts of survivors, arguing that no matter how evocative or compelling eyewitness statements might be, they are only recollections of individuals. People retell what is most interesting, or what remains brightest in the memory. Such advocates remind us that 'truth' is elusive, provisional. Memories are flawed, focal points limited, survivor accounts questionable. I trace through documents. Histories of words recorded. Slip back in time, tracking the source of smoke to the fire itself.

I find Article 58, 'Causes for imprisonment': Anyone opposing the incoming occupation, anyone serving a counter-revolutionary goal, any dissident, White Army combatant or member of the opposition party, is an enemy of the state. Soldiers returning from the front are imprisoned. Their crime? Not dying in defence of the motherland. The list of 'offences' includes treason, non-reporting of treason, flight when charged with treason. Trials are held *in absentia*. The accused are found guilty of terrorism, involvement with international collaborators, occupying state property, releasing intelligence, undermining state industry, compromising transportation or communications, insurrection, subversion, provocation, agitation, and non-reporting of such activities. For the betterment of the State. Records list prisoners of all races and religions. Prisoners include a United Nations of poets, artists, scientists, educators, intellectuals, spiritual leaders, free-thinkers. The cream of the crop. Although the Second World War ended in early September of 1945, most Gulag concentration camps remained operational until 1953 and were only closed following Stalin's death. Others continued until the 1960s, some, much longer. Many claim that the Gulag persists.

In 2012, two members of the band Pussy Riot were sentenced to what some call the Gulag. In 1954, following Stalin's death, many prisons in the Gulag system were transformed into 'corrective labour camps'. By 1961, the Mordovia camps primarily handled those convicted of political crimes. Pussy Riot's music champions feminism, LGBTQ+ rights and opposition to Putin's policies, including his links to the Russian Orthodox Church. Convicted of 'hooliganism', Nadezhda Tolokonnikova was sentenced to Mordovia and Maria Alyokhina to Perm. Two years each. One supporter tweeted that those were the cruellest camps in the prison system.

Some traces of the old Gulag remain, although photographic evidence is scarce. Many camps were ordered bulldozed over.

The trail grows elusive when winding through a turbulence of different languages, varying accounts. It was with remarkable foresight that, in 1945, Eisenhower, Allied Commander in Chief, after visiting the Ohrdruf Nazi concentration camp, ordered members of the U.S. military, as well as reporters and filmmakers, to record the atrocities. No such records were made of the Gulag.

There are still the names. Chermkhovo, Chita, Inta, Irkutsk, Kadala, Kolyma, Komsomolsk, Krasnoyarsk, Muli, Novosibirsk, Poshet, Suchan, Taiseta, Vladivostok, Voroshilov, Vorkuta, and perhaps a thousand more. What's in a name? Gulag. *Glavnoe upravlenie ispravitel'notrudovykh lagereĭ*—the chief administration of corrective labour camps. Solzhenitsyn dubbed it the 'Gulag Archipelago', citing prisons stretching in a chain of 'islands' across Siberia. Solzhenitsyn estimates some 50 million people passed through, during his time. Past prisoners include: Mikhail Bakhtin, literary theorist; Menachem Begin, later prime minister of Israel; Andrei Sakharov, dissident nuclear physicist; Alekanders Pelēcis, poet. Legions of others are recorded. Pelēcis survived. His *Siberia Book (Sibirijas Grāmata)* documents the horrors.

My uncle was a nineteen-year-old farm boy when he was incarcerated. He was stripped, except for shirt, shoes, trousers. All buttons, belts, zippers removed. A deliberate humiliation. Shipped to the Gulag with thousands of others, jammed in cattle cars. His letters arrived in the mid-1950s, written on pulp-paper, folded into makeshift triangular envelopes. I recall how our family tried to send packets of non-perishable food, tobacco, anything to improve his circumstances. It made little difference. The packets never seemed to arrive. We guessed that the care packages were taken by guards. He was imprisoned, then died, long after the war ended.

In the old country, my father's family raised sugar beets. In Canada, he switched to carpentry. He regularly tuned up and repaired our old sedan, always ready to make a run for it. My mother continued as a bookkeeper at the Wedgewood Restaurant near the intersection of Jane and Bloor. She kept abundant preserves in the cold cellar, just in case. Both wondered why *they* had lived, when so many others had died. Shell shock rattled their minds. I caught the darkness drinking from their cup. My uncle's correspondences acknowledged our letters, but never our packets.

Some have condemned the great silence, the untenable muteness, in the face of millions dead. Regimes of 'truth' raise greater disparities than agreements. In the late 1980s, one eminent historian cited 20 million dead. A Ukrainian investigator named 32.5 million dead. A British-Polish historian cited 50 million dead excluding war losses. A U.S. historian lists death counts of 56 to 62 million, with some 50 million specifically under Stalin. The Russian Secret Police place the number at 1.6 million. Take it or leave it. Thubron reports that upon departing Vorkuta, he tripped on a stone into which someone had scratched the following message: 'I was exiled in 1949, and my father died here in 1942. Remember us.'

Smoke on the water. A syntax of death. Fortunes of war. Letters from overseas. My parents read my uncle's letters and wept. And now the bundle of triangulated notes has fallen into my hands. 'Can you send me something?' Letters sent from the Irkutsk Region. Taiseta. One island in the Gulag Archipelago.

It has been a week since I sent my last letter to you. I beg your pardon for not writing sooner, but I believe you understand the condition I have fallen into. It would be especially helpful if you could send me a small packet. It is the third day that I've gone to bed without eating. I await a crust of bread, but my group has been disregarded. I fear the worst. Perhaps you've already sent me something. I can't be certain. Many packets arriving are held for inspection. I fear many are not released. Something practical would make a big difference, a bag of macaroni perhaps. Say hello to our neighbours and friends. Good-bye for now. Be in good health. Please send more letters. I await impatiently for your replies. If I ever see you again, I will press your warm hand against my face and embrace it endlessly. I will shower countless kisses onto your gentle cheek. I await your reply.

Yours, Peter

Today I am reading an excerpt from a journal kept by Jacques Rossi. Born to a wealthy French family, he joined the Communist Party, worked abroad, but was ordered to return to Moscow after the civil war in Spain. Falsely accused of Fascism, he was exiled to Siberia. A survivor, he wrote a detailed account, beginning with a discovery by his work gang of a man sitting alone in the snow. An accompanying guard, frustrated at the man's lack of movement, coaxed him with the butt of his rifle. The man toppled over. He'd been dead a while. The guard bent over the corpse, pulled away a ragged scarf. On each side of his neck, the veins were opened. Lifting the man's jacket revealed two large wounds where his kidneys had been. He was a 'cow', as such victims are named. Callous inmates sometimes invited naïve, newly arrived prisoners on an 'escape'. They'd describe a detailed getaway plan. On a given day, they'd trek past the barbed-wire enclosure on some routine work detail, beyond the view of the machine-gun turrets. They'd break down into smaller groups moving deeper into the forest, ostensibly to retrieve pre-cut logs. Routine labour. The newcomers were not yet aware that they were surrounded by a thousand kilometres of frozen muskeg. There was no escape. Ignoring the log detail, the malefactors departed with the 'cow', snuffed him, slit his throat, consumed his blood and kidneys. Fire and smoke would betray their location to the guard waiting back at the perimeter. They harvested what could be ingested without cooking. No smoke. Only the sound of death muffled by green forest depths.

The setting sun's rays slant through my window. My incense joss stick has abruptly expired. I understand that there are two pasts: one actual and the other inscribed. Among some people, it is believed that both good *and* evil rule the world. Over the span of a year, twelve forms of human malevolence or stupidity arise, one for each month. Once a year, the Bardo Chham must be danced to dispel the senseless evil.

When the Pequat were massacred at Mystic River, when a black haze arose over Birkenau, when the bomb touched the pavement of Nagasaki, when the blockbusters levelled Dresden, when napalm cascaded over Trang Bang, when bulldozers buried mass graves in Beirut, when machine-gun paramilitants burst into prayer meetings in Chiapas, when white phosphorous swept Fallujah, there was always smoke rising in a tell-tale trail. But, when those in the Siberian Gulag passed into death with a single foggy breath, there was only silence.

It is the summer solstice. It always begins here, near the river, now that it is summer once again, and the warm solstice night envelops our huddled bodies. We've met here each year, to embrace, dance and sing around campfires of hospitality. Here, we reassert ourselves, give thanks, share stories. It's here that the wheel of time pauses before turning again. After sunset, we wander from campfire to campfire, find ourselves in small groups, among old friends, singing, in circles, around fire-licked logs, our words returning to times past or spinning ahead to imagined futures. Tranquil smoke billows catch moonlight, but, I cannot forget Attawapiskat. We rest beneath the moth-eaten star-blanket, a bit worse for the wear. The song-filled night shifts beyond the canopy of oaks and tall maples. I've said this before, but when we return to this place each year, we return to endless beginnings and are transformed, yet still remain the same, momentarily running fingers through smoke-filled hair, through drifts of summer moments linking years not quite forgotten, retrieved from dusty temporal pockets. The rising smoke shares our unspoken desires, passions, anxieties, dreams. Whenever we gather on the shortest night of the year, we become timeless within the heat and heart of summer. The sun burns a course through its highest path. Days are at their longest. I've returned to this place from before the time I could walk. It was here that my extended family emerged. My adopted aunt Julie, who grasped my upraised hands and led me as I learned to walk, stepping through the green, sun-kissed morning. Half a century later, I stood by her hospital bed, stroking ashen hair swept across her sleeping eyes. She would never reawaken, never again walk with me in the green morning.

It was here that I discovered the dangerous strength of silent water. Playing barefoot by the muddy banks as my godfather and father entered into animated debate over things that mattered then, I slipped into the curving flow, knowing only that I couldn't swim as a whirlpool swiftly pulled me from the shore, cast me into a yawning circle. I flutter-kicked, swept my arms, attempted to remain afloat. In a single lifetime, we are granted rare moments of clarity which grip us unexpectedly and will not be denied. As the whirlpool swept me round its perimeter, I took cold comfort in the fact that I would soon pass back to shore, past the weeping willow branches that hung nearly to the water, back to the muddy bank. But, in grasping for the willows, my hands slipped, too wet to gain a firm grip against the cycling current, and as I swept past the bank, I could not regain footing on the slippery muck, and so was whirled again into the black river flow. On my second turn around, I felt myself weakening, gripped by the cold knowledge that I would not survive another full circle. Sinking in silence, swept under the muddy stream, I glimpsed the shoreline, my godfather's and father's arms moving in animated discussion, I struggled to break surface, and for an instant, cried a yelp. Afterwards, I sat well away from the bank, my father scolding me, wrapping a grey blanket around my shoulders. The campfire drifted smoke nearby. It is here on the shores of this river that we often meet, ever returning on the longest day, cycling through our years, gathering for one evening with old friends, confirming our existences, looking to indefinite futures.

But this year, I am not with those others gathered by the river. This year, I am sequestered, in my room, alone with recurrent thoughts. The joss stick has burned out. I turn my forehead to the sky and remind myself that words recalling things past are only smoke, they are not the things themselves.

ACKNOWLEDGEMENTS

Huge thanks to publishers and editors who recognized merit in my fictions and chose to publish them. Special thanks to Tim and Elke Inkster and Stephanie Small at the Porcupine's Quill. I am honoured and deeply grateful.

Warm appreciation to Hal Jaffe at *Fiction International*, who published a version of 'Cinderella Pecadilla', as well as 'Fluid Mechanics: Cold Vodka, Cold Blood' (a modified version of 'Understanding the Sounds You Hear').

Warmest thanks to both Bev Daurio and Richard Truhlar who solicited my writing and edited anthologies of short fiction for Tekst Editions (Toronto) featuring early versions of 'Understanding the Sounds You Hear' and 'Watch, Watching', among other pieces.

Special thanks to Joyce Carol Oates who invited me to send material to *The Ontario Review* (Princeton University) which published an earlier version of 'Watch, Watching'.

And thanks to the Josephine Writers workshop and all those who have advised me and encouraged me. I am humbled and thankful.